FIRE ON THE MOUNTAIN

To Moira —

dearest God-daughter —

with much love

Ilse

FIRE ON THE MOUNTAIN

A Journey Through Time

Irene B. Seeland

CONTENTS

To Helen Wambach, who opened
the Doors to the Past

To Erling, who opened the Path
to the Future

To all my Travel Companions,
Past, Present, and Future

With Love, Gratitude, and Hope

ACKNOWLEDGEMENTS

My thanks and gratitude to those who helped this little book to be what it is:

Linda DeVore for her thoughtful editing work and her encouraging comments;

Christine Moore who took my very rough sketches, some old photos and picture-postcards and from them created delicate works of art;

Donna Christie who lovingly and carefully proofread and corrected the final manuscript;

Christopher Thunberg for his many trips to the mountain to get the perfect picture;

And **Xlibris** for being there and making it all possible!

PROLOGUE

The hawk circled in the clear autumn air, high above the hillsides already turning gold and red. The old woman leaned her head against the back of the chair and let the sun warm her. The petunias in the old-fashioned stone containers swayed in the light breeze fragrant with the scent of the tall pine trees standing like ancient guardians below the big white house on the mountainside.

She could hear the laughter and the sounds of the children running and playing in the gardens behind the house, and she smiled. Three generations—she had witnessed them all growing up, learning, loving, suffering, reaching out into the world and embracing it—all her friends, their children, and now their children's children. It had been a very rich life.

She smiled and looked at the sun lighting up her hands, the skin thin and transparent like parchment. A butterfly tumbled through one of the terrace arches and lit upon the flowers. It was a blue swallowtail and it sat quietly, its wings trembling in the sunlight, shimmering like jewels.

She heard footsteps coming quickly through the room adjacent to the terrace, and a small voice whispered behind her chair: "Gran, are you asleep?"

She smiled and turned. "No, sweetheart, just resting. Come and see the beautiful butterfly that came to visit me," and she pointed to the flowers.

The little girl, her small pointed face serious under brown ringlets, tiptoed closer. For a little while they both watched in silence, the old woman and the little girl. Then the butterfly rose and dropped away, down to the flowers spreading in profusion in the garden below the terrace. The little girl sat beside her, looking at her intently. "Gran, how old do people have to be when they die?"

The old woman looked at her with surprise. "Child, what made you think about that?"

"I asked Dad about his father, and he said he had died real young. I thought only old people die."

"Little friend, most of the time, people are quite old and tired and their bodies worn out from long lives and years of work and care before they decide to leave them. But sometimes, and we don't always understand why, young people and even children die—some of them from a sudden illness, some of them through accidents. It happens, though not very often."

"But those that die young, Gran, what happens to them then? They had no chance to grow up and learn and go to work and have children. Will they have another chance?"

"Some people believe we have many chances, Annie, that we are born many times, and in many different cultures, to learn greater wisdom and love for others. And if we make mistakes, we have a chance to make it right again, in the same life or in another."

"Do you believe that, too, Gran?" The child looked at her wistfully. "And if it is true, why don't we remember who we were before?"

"We do sometimes, but only when it is helpful for us to do so. It is often hard enough to live with the memories of one lifetime. If we remembered them all, it would quite overwhelm us, I think. But something in us always remembers the lessons we learned, and that is probably all we really need to remember."

"Do you remember me from some other time, Gran? Do people who love each other come together again? Will I always be your granddaughter, again and again?"

"Now wouldn't that be boring?" The old woman sat up and laughed. "How about sometimes you would be my Gran, or my son, or just a really good friend? So that way we could have all different kinds of fun together."

"I'm glad this time you are my Gran, though," the little voice concluded with satisfaction, and bending towards the old woman, the child delivered a swift kiss on her wrinkled cheek and skipped off. The old woman leaned back and smiled to herself. She let her thoughts travel back in time to her own childhood and to other important times in her life that stood out clearly in her mind. And as she remembered them, the other, older memories came flooding . . . .

CHAPTER ONE

The Soldiers

The little girl sat very quietly in the corner of the cobblestone back yard. The old house sheltered her from the occasional sharp gusts of the April wind, and when the sun escaped from the heavy white clouds, it was quite warm. She hugged her doll closer and pulled the little jacket over its soft little body. Her skinny legs began to hurt from sitting so long in one position, but she did not want to move for fear of waking her doll child.

She could hear the boys shouting and running in the orchard behind the house. They were hiding behind the trunks of the old cherry trees, and occasionally they burst out in loud shouts, imitating volleys of shots from their rifles made from windfall branches and old pieces of string.

The little girl was listening to the chirping of the sparrows in the hedge separating the house from the neighbor's garden. There were four of them hopping restlessly about. She remembered the sound of their chirping from the day when, after the long winter illness, her mother had picked her up and taken her to the window to show her the pink clouds of the cherry trees in bloom and the high, clear blue sky. The wind had been soft and full of sweet smells and had blown the curtains like veils into the room.

It had felt so good to feel the wind again. All winter while she had been in bed, her chest had hurt so much, and each time when she had had to cough, she had been afraid of the sharp pain. The doctor had come twice a week, and he and her mother had talked in soft voices by the window. Much of the time she had felt so sleepy and far away that she did not hear what they said, but once she had heard the word "pneumonia" and somehow she knew it was something bad.

At night, she had often awakened from the wailing of the air raid sirens, and her mother had come and wrapped her in her blanket and carried her into the cellar where she and her sister and grandmother and the other people from the house would sit and listen to the droning of the bombers for a long time. There was always fear in the cellar—she could nearly taste it—and people would whisper, "Last week they bombed Berlin again," or "My sister wrote me there is not much left of Hamburg." When the bombers returned from their destination, she could hear a difference in the way they sounded, lighter somehow, and eager to go home. In the past weeks they had had to go into the cellar nearly every night, and people were quieter and more afraid.

The little girl took a deep breath, cherishing the fact that there was no pain now in her chest. She slowly put the baby doll into the little cardboard box her mother had so carefully fitted with a pretty pink and white piece of fabric and even a little pillow.

She considered the meager store of food her mother had been able to give her for her play today—a handful of oatmeal, a little paper bag with raisins, and a cup of carrot slices. She mixed them carefully in a little pan and then went to fetch some water from the faucet by the basement door. The faucet was dripping slowly, and on the ground, a little patch of moss, soft and dark green, looked like a piece of velvet. The little girl ran her fingers over it. It felt like velvet too. She knew, because she had a dark blue velvet dress, just like her older sister, with little pink and light blue flowers embroidered on the front yoke.

She returned to her sun-warmed corner and stirred the porridge. Then she set out four small plates, collected four little branches from the orchard and placed them neatly beside the plates. She often helped her mother set the table, so she knew where to put spoons and knives and forks.

Then she stood up and called out to the boys, "Come and get lunch!" She had to call three times to be heard over their shouting and shooting. There were three of them, all with bright eyes and high color in their faces. Their clothes showed signs of frequent mending and their leather boots were worn and patched.

They sat down eagerly around the meager fare and, scooping with branches and fingers, finished the sticky cold porridge quickly. "Is there no more?" the smallest of them asked, looking among the utensils the little girl had meticulously arranged on an imaginary stove.

"It is all mother could spare," she said apologetically. The tallest of them bowed politely from his waist, in an imitation of what he must have seen his father do in company. "Thank you for the fine meal," he said. "It was quite delicious."

The little girl giggled. She looked up admiringly at him. She loved the way the sun lit up his hair, like real gold, just like the picture of the prince in the fairy tale book her aunt had brought her for Christmas. He had much the same looks as that prince, she thought; maybe he was a prince in disguise.

Then she giggled again. She knew too well that he was only the boy downstairs, living with his mother and old grandfather on the ground floor of the big white house. His father, like all their fathers, was gone to war. Fathers returned rarely and only for a few days, tired, quiet men, unwilling to speak, hugging their children close with worried, pained eyes, only to leave again while their wives stayed behind with frozen faces, trying to hide the fear.

The boys stood, picking up their makeshift rifles, shouldered them and, standing in line one behind the other, started to count: "One, two, three, four . . . ." The tall boy turned around, being the leader by age, size, and inner authority. "Goodbye, woman," he said, his voice becoming suddenly deeper, "we are going off to war again. But," and here his voice lifted again, "we shall be back soon."

The little girl looked at him, suddenly feeling cold, taking her baby doll from its bed and holding it close, very close. Her chest was feeling tight and it was hard to breathe and to swallow. The boys turned and began marching, one, two, one, two . . . .

She suddenly felt tears running down her cheeks and she buried her face in the body of the baby doll. A thought was running in her head, over and over: They will never come back, I will never see any of them again . . . .

*　　*　　*

Britain, circa 50 BC

Etta stood in the doorway, hugging the child close to her. The rain was falling softly just outside the roof overhang. The fog that had hidden the world all morning was still hanging in the treetops and bushes but had become a little lighter on the ground. She looked down at the baby. He was asleep, breathing lightly, his eyelashes strangely dark on his light skin. Etta shifted him to her other arm. "He is getting heavy," she thought and smiled. "Such a little one and getting heavy already."

Her eyes followed the road. There were only a few other huts between hers and the encroaching woods. The village was quiet, very quiet. There were none of the familiar sounds of everyday activities. The women and children were staying hidden inside, feeling vulnerable and afraid after the men had left the village before daybreak.

Only the old tanner, lame and bent with age, had stayed behind, too frail to go with the others. He was sitting quietly on the doorstep of his hut at the end of the road. Etta could barely make out his shape in the dimness of the rainy day. She could more easily see his dog, a strangely white creature, bony and bent like his master. He appeared asleep, stretched out with his head resting on his front paws. But Etta knew that any strange sound or any sign of the men returning would instantly bring him to his legs.

The boy who watched the goats out on the hillsides at the other side of the small wood had come running into the village at dusk yesterday, telling of watch fires down where the river left their small valley.

The men had gathered quickly and quietly in the meeting house and had spent much of the night talking about whether they should stay in the village, hoping that rain and fog would hide the small path leading off the river road to their village, or go to the edge of the woods and watch to see if the Roman soldiers would turn off from their usual travels by the river. The soldiers had traveled up the river road much of the past year, but so far they had not disturbed the little hamlet.

One of the men, Perre, a small, dark-haired man with restless eyes, had suggested that they send a scout to find out how many soldiers there were this time. Maybe if there were few enough, the men could attack the Romans in the night and come away with weapons and food and silver.

Lathan, the druid priest had shaken his head. He had come to live with them last winter after having been lost outside the woods in a heavy snowstorm. He would have died if Freder and his hunting dog had not found the still figure huddled against an ancient oak. He had raised his clear voice and told them that the Romans nearly always traveled in strong numbers. "They are a well-trained army," he had said, "with strong leaders and good weapons." And Freder, who had told Etta about the meeting, had smiled. "He was kind enough not to say, 'Not like your little ragtag band of starved peasants.'"

Etta wondered again at the strange friendship that had developed between the tall, slim man whose light brown hair curled tightly around his fine-boned head like a cap, whose clear gray eyes had a gaze that often seemed to look into far distances, and Freder, strong and well muscled, with blond hair falling well to his shoulders, with a voice that carried far when he cared to use it in the village meetings.

She had happily moved in with Freder when her own father had finally died. The years of suffering from the wasting illness had left the strong blacksmith only a shadow of his former self. Although Freder and she had been lovers for a while, she had not wanted to leave her father, who had remained a widower since the death of her mother at her birth. He had never taken another woman into the house. During her early years, he had given Etta to his sister to nurse and care for the little red-haired sprite that had come from the strange liaison of the big, heavy-boned man with the bushy black hair and the heavy eyebrows that nearly hid his bright blue eyes and the slight red-haired woman whom he had brought home one day from a trip to the market town.

He had never told Etta where her mother had come from, but she had wondered at times if she had not been a runaway slave whom her father had taken to their remote village, where nobody would come looking for her. The villagers had found her a shy girl, friendly when spoken to. But she had done little to make friends with the other women in the village. Etta's aunt Meri, big-boned like her father, with the same strong hair and bright blue eyes, had told Etta these things about her mother.

Meri had been with Etta's mother during her long child labor, she served the women in the village in that way. The woman had labored for two days in great pain, and in the end had given birth to the baby with her last strength, failing quickly in a flood of bleeding that no skill of Meri's had had any power to stop.

Etta had grown up strong and well-built like her father, and only her radiant red hair had set her aside as the child of the outsider who had entered their small, closed community.

Etta looked again at her son. He had Freder's strong body but his hair was very fair, lying close to his well-rounded head. The moisture in the air had made little droplets on the rough blanket that Etta had wrapped him in before taking up her vigil for the return of the men.

She could hear Meta, Freder's mother, moving in the house behind her, preparing the noon meal for Kirra and Ceil, Freder's younger sister and brother. She stepped back into the house, grateful for the warmth of the cooking fire on the great kitchen hearth. Standing so long in the cold, she was stiff from the clammy air and her arms hurt from holding the boy quietly for so long. She gently laid the baby in the cradle close by the fire, and sipped the hot soup from the bowl that Meta handed her.

She loved Meta, the quiet gray-haired widow of the former headman of the village, who had taken kindly to the little red-haired daughter of the stranger. Etta had often wondered if her acceptance by the villagers had not been a result of Meta's kindness to her. She had fallen in love with Freder while still a young girl, awkward with the sudden growth of her body, and had sought advice and comfort from the motherly older woman.

She sat for a while by the fire, letting the warmth seep into her damp clothes and her stiff joints. The children, Kirra, in her twelfth year, and Ceil, going on ten and wanting to be fourteen so he could have gone with the men, were talking, their voices hushed like everyone's today, as if in this way their village in its quietness would remain hidden from the eyes of the soldiers traveling up river. A sudden feeling of restlessness made Etta rise again. She took the shawl that had been drying by the fire and, wrapping it tightly around her, returned to her watching post in the doorway.

At that moment, she saw the tanner's dog lift his white head and raise himself stiffly to his legs. Etta was waiting to see him move down the road, tail wagging to greet the returning men, but with sudden dread, she saw his posture change to a crouch, and even from her position, she could hear his low grumbling growl that was his signal that strangers were coming to the village.

Etta's heart suddenly seemed to beat in her throat. Her eyes still could not penetrate the path leading into the woods at the end of the village, and the fog muffled most sounds, but she thought she heard the jingling of horse harnesses. None of the men had taken any horses. They had planned to stay quietly in the woods, hidden and intending to fight only if the soldiers showed any sign of veering off their usual path.

She stood frozen on the doorstep as she watched first one and then two more horses emerge from the path in the wood, tall, well muscled horses, not the little skinny nags of the villagers.

The riders were tall and well built too, and dressed in the metal and leather armor of the Roman army. The first one, clearly the leader by stature and the mark of his red cloak, turned as he saw the houses emerge from the fog, and raised his arm in a signal to stop the others. Etta could see behind him a troop of soldiers, marching in formation, about twenty men.

Etta thought with pity and anger of the small band of the village men, who had left in the cold, damp dawn, dressed in their threadbare clothes, with whatever weapons they had been able to contrive. Only Freder had a real sword, given to him by his father. The others had taken knives and axes, and some their bows and arrows.

There was no sign of any of the village men within this group, and Etta's heart sank. The officer had seen her in the doorway and rode his horse up through the center of the hamlet, careless of the muddy puddles, reining his horse in only a few feet away from Etta.

She now could see his face clearly, a strong face with an aquiline nose and close-cropped dark hair showing under his helmet. He turned to the other riders behind him, motioning them to draw up behind him and giving some order in a strange but melodious language. He pointed to the shivering woman in the doorway.

One of the other two riders was not armored, but dressed in breeches of good brown cloth and a dark brown cloak held by a copper brooch of strange design. He measured Etta with dark eyes and addressed her in her own language, though with a strange accent that made him hard to understand.

"Where is the headman of the village, woman," he asked her, "and where are the other men?" he added, realizing that their arrival in the village had not brought out any people, just an occasional wan face of woman or child peering forth from behind doorways or window shutters.

Etta's mind was racing. What had happened to their men and how had the soldiers gotten to the village without a battle?

"They went to hunt for meat this morning," she said, trying to keep her fear from her voice. "They may be back by night or be gone for a few days if the hunt is poor. Winter is coming and the harvest has been bad. We need the meat for the winter."

She noticed the frown on the face of the first officer, who stared at her as if trying to read her thoughts. He turned and spoke quietly to the other officer behind him, who in turn shouted orders at the soldiers ranged behind him. The second officer was an older man, short and heavy of build, with gray, short-cropped hair that showed unruly after he had taken off his helmet to run his hand over his head. His eyes were those of a man very tired or in pain.

Ten soldiers separated from the troop and, with swords drawn, began to search the huts of the village. Etta could hear women screaming in fear as the soldiers entered, but when the soldiers brought the inhabitants out of the huts, nobody appeared hurt. The soldiers marched the women to the center of the village, and the man in the brown cloak went to talk to them.

It was then that Etta realized that her story of the hunt would not stand up long, because the other women would either tell the truth or make up their own lies.

The man in the cloak returned shortly to the younger officer to report what he had gathered from talking to the women. Etta saw the officer smile grimly. His answer was long, but he fixed his eyes on Etta as he was talking, and continued to stare at her as the man in brown turned to her.

"If those men who attacked us back there by the woods were your men, they showed poor judgment in trying to fight Roman soldiers. There are none of them left alive except one who seems to be a druid priest, and he is wounded badly and not expected to live. We will take whatever food we can use from your village, and we will take you and two other women with us as payment for the trouble your men caused us this morning. We will not burn down your village, seeing that winter is close, but the others better remember that it is foolish and useless to attack the Roman army."

Etta stared at the officers and the man in brown. She could feel her heart beating hard in her chest, and her throat was so tight that it was difficult to bring out the question she needed to ask most: "Was there a man with a sword among them?" she whispered. "Tall and blond, and with a sword?"

The man in brown turned to the younger officer, who in turn raised a questioning eyebrow at the older officer who was looking at Etta with a strange expression, in which wariness seemed mixed with pity. He spoke quietly and the man in brown turned back. "He was the one who gave us much trouble, being a strong fighter and brave, but not skilled in using a sword. He died quickly and cleanly, stabbed through the heart."

Etta's heart seemed to contract with a piercing pain so strong that she dared not breathe. "Freder," she thought, "oh, Freder, now you will never come back, never see your son grow up strong and beautiful, never make love to me, never hold me again when I am sad," and the immensity of her loss wanted to overwhelm her. But she was resolved not to cry in front of these strange men who had come and destroyed her life and that of her son, and had left the world an empty grayness, as gray and shapeless as this endless cursed fog that had not even served to save her man.

She had felt for a while that Meta was standing behind her in the doorway, and the sudden crying of the baby brought her back from the grayness of her frozen grief to the demands and reality of life.

Meta stepped forward, handing her the baby, and addressed the officer in charge. "Let her stay," she said quietly. "She has a small babe to feed and her heart is heavy. She will be of little use to you, and though I am older, I am still strong enough to do hard work and be a good servant for many years to come."

The officer looked at her with disbelief as her words were translated. He hesitated for a moment, then shook his head.

"The young one will come with us, and two other women of serviceable age." He quickly turned to the older officer and gave orders, on which the soldiers re-entered the houses to search them for their meager stores of food. Etta stood frozen in the doorway, her body cold and stiff as if life were no longer pulsing through it. Then with sudden resolution, she turned and pressed the baby into Meta's arms. "Take him," she whispered. "He is your son's son; he will grow up to be like him. Take him and raise him for me, and if I can, I will come back to you both."

The man in brown had been watching her all this while and spoke to her again.

"Go and take some of your belongings," he said, not unkindly, "and bring some warm clothing. We travel fast and sleep in tents, and winter is coming."

Etta stared at him, finding it hard to understand what he was saying, but Meta turned back into the house and returned shortly with her own warm cloak and whatever clothes she had been able to find. Etta accepted the bundle quietly, and only when the man in brown told her to come and join the other two women already wailing and crying in the village center did she rouse herself enough to embrace Meta, who was holding the baby, tears running quietly down her face.

"Call him Freder," she whispered, "and tell him about his mother and father," and suddenly at the thought of her son growing up motherless like herself, she cried out aloud, "Oh, Goddess, protect him in your mercy," and pulled her shawl over her head as if in mourning.

The troop fell back into formation and began to march back

on the small road that led through the woods to the river. Etta walked with the other women, who were still sobbing and calling on the goddess to protect them. Nell, the younger of the two, had been living with her parents and older brother and had come into womanhood only in the past year. She was a slight girl with a pale face and a somewhat stooped posture, but a kind disposition. The other, Kara, a dark-haired woman of strong build, had been widowed in the past winter when her man had been killed by a falling tree, and she had no children.

Etta turned to them and put her arm around the younger one. "Come, Nell," she said gently, "they have not treated us ill so far. They could have killed us all or burned down the village. They will put us to service and maybe, after a while, they will let us go home again."

Kara turned at her angrily. "Don't you know anything about Roman soldiers?" she whispered hoarsely. "They take women to serve them as whores and then sell them as slaves when they are tired of them." Nell cried out again at this, and Etta turned away in anger and despair.

They reached the woods quickly and passed through them, the women walking behind the soldiers, barely able to keep up to their trained speed. When they came to the edge of the trees where the path was leading down to the river, Etta turned to search for any signs of the battle, but the fog and the growing dimness of the late afternoon made it impossible to see anything but dripping branches and wet leaves, with their smell of mold and decay.

By nightfall they reached the campsite of the soldiers further up the river, and the man in brown pointed to a small tent for the women to sleep in. A soldier brought some hot stew and hard bread and a leather skin of sour wine, and Etta, in spite of her sorrow, had to smile; she thought to herself that the proud Roman army did not live much better than poor farmers. The tent was damp, and the blankets they had found in a corner were thin and smelled of mold and sweat.

The three women sat quietly together, too tired and crushed

by the day's events to feel any desire to talk. It was dark now, and the soldiers sat around their fires. There were many more in the camp than the small troop that had come to Etta's village. They seemed a well-trained and disciplined group and, so far, none had made any attempt to harass the women.

Nell, seeing that she was not in immediate danger of becoming the victim of Roman soldiers, had finally cried herself to sleep and Kara, grumbling and muttering, had joined her, lying close to her to gain whatever warmth could be had from one another in this cold damp autumn night. Etta sat huddled by the tent entrance staring into the dark. She was thinking of Freder and the men and the hopeless battle they had fought to protect their small village, and she wondered if it would not have been wiser for them to stay in the village and give the Romans what they wanted.

And then she knew that it was not in the nature of men to sit by and have their women and property taken from them without battle. None of them could have gone on living, feeling like men, and most would have preferred an honorable death in battle. She sighed and turned to find a corner away from the wind that had started to blow in short little gusts, blowing away the fog and even beginning to clear the sky so that an occasional star and a glimmer of moonlight showed in the heavens.

Suddenly she saw a figure step out from one of the soldiers' tents and make his way across the camp area to her tent. For a moment she was afraid and wondered if Kara had been right and one of the soldiers was coming to find his pleasure with one of them. But then she recognized the man in brown who strode up and bent down to her. "Do you have any healing skills?" he asked briskly.

Etta looked at him. "I know something of herbs and how to set broken bones," she answered quietly, "and I know something of childbirth," she added and had to smile. The man in brown smiled, too. "Not much need for that in this army," he said, "but if you have skill with wounds and fevers, you can come and look at that priest who was with the men from your village. He got a bad sword cut to his head, and he is raving and his fever is high."

Etta stared at him. "Lathan," she whispered, "Goddess, Lathan, he is alive!" and then she remembered that the officer had told her this earlier in the day, but she had not heard it in her despair over Freder's death. "I will come," she said, "but I have none of my healing herbs with me."

"We have a medic with us," the brown man said. "Tell me what you need and I will ask him for you."

They quickly walked to the center of the camp and the brown-cloaked man showed her to a large tent where several injured men were stretched out on cots on the floor. She recognized Lathan's long thin figure and knelt by him. His face was flushed and his eyes bright and wild. He was tossing restlessly and murmured words in a language Etta had never heard him use before. The wound was at the side of his head, and although it seemed to have bled heavily, it had not injured the bones, as Etta's quick fingers reassured her. But she knew that even a glancing stroke to the head could kill or cause injury to the brain.

Lathan, although awake, did not seem to recognize her or his surroundings. She turned and asked the man in brown for some water and clean linen, with which she began to wash the crusted blood from Lathan's hair. She found that the scalp was cut deeply but cleanly, and wished that she had some way to keep the hair out of the wound. The man in brown had watched her closely and suddenly said, "Who is this man? He is not one of yours. He carries the insignia of a druid priest, yet he speaks a tongue that is not from these parts."

"I do not know where he is from." Etta turned and looked at him. "My man found him half frozen in a snowstorm in the woods last winter and he nearly died. Then he stayed with us for a while and became our friend. He told us that he was a druid and he knows the rituals and the prayers. He has traveled much and we loved to listen to his tales from faraway places. And he knows songs from many lands."

Suddenly Etta broke into tears, remembering the evenings when she and Freder and Meta had sat by the fire listening to Lathan's tales or hearing his rich, clear voice sing songs full of magic and beauty.

The man in brown laid his hand over Etta's arm. "Tell me about your man," he said quietly.

Etta shook her head. "I cannot," she said, "not yet, but I thank you for your kindness. What is your name?" she asked as an afterthought, realizing she had called him "the man in brown" in her mind ever since earlier in the day—which now seemed a lifetime away.

He smiled. "My name is Marius," he said, "Marius Tortellius, the son of a Roman soldier . . . and a Saxon slave," he added with a bitter smile. "What is yours?"

"Etta," she said simply, and then added," daughter of Angus, the blacksmith, and woman to Freder the headman," and then the tears began to roll down her face again.

"Well, Etta," said Marius kindly, "take care of your friend here and stay with him if you like. I will send the medic to bring you whatever medicines we have for fevers." With that, he rose and left the tent.

For three nights and days Etta stayed with Lathan. The soldiers broke camp in the morning, and Lathan and the other wounded were loaded in two carts pulled by mules. Etta, through intercession by Marius, traveled with Lathan in the cart. On the evening of the third day, Lathan looked at Etta with clear eyes and whispered her name.

She bent over him. "Lathan," she said, "oh, Lathan, what happened to you all?"

"It was ill luck and human greed," he said bitterly. "That fool Perre thought to sneak down before dawn to steal some food from the Roman camp and got caught. After that, it was a question of time until they would find out from him that he was not alone and then find us and slaughter us. We were no match for them; we never had a chance. But your man fought bravely and fiercely," he added and looked at Etta with compassion.

She told him briefly what had happened in the village and, under his kind eyes, found it hard not to start weeping again.

"Poor Etta," he said softly, "and poor little babe." Then, bracing himself, he sat up with some of his old energy. "Can you find this man Marius you told me about?" he asked. "He may be able to help us. I have some Roman friends, and if he can help me to talk to the commanding officer, he may be willing to release us."

Etta stared at him in disbelief. "You have Roman friends?" she asked.

Lathan smiled. "I have friends in many countries, Etta," he said quietly. "But you and Freder and Meta had become my family."

After the soldiers made camp in the evening Etta set out to find Marius and, as usual, found him in the company of the two officers whose names and history she had learned from him.

The younger but senior officer, Aurelius Tertius, was the youngest son of a Roman senator; the older, Phillipus Ardenius was a veteran of many battles of the Roman army. As Etta approached them, Marius rose to greet her. "How is your friend," he asked, "and how are you?"

Etta smiled. "His fever has broken and his mind is clear again. He wishes to speak to you, because he says he has some Roman friends and hopes that he can appeal to the officers here to send them news of his misfortunes."

Marius looked at her quizzically. "Are you sure his head is clear?" he asked with raised eyebrows. For a moment Etta's own doubts showed, but then she pleaded, "Please," she said, "come and talk to him yourself. You will see."

When Marius entered the tent of the wounded soldiers, Lathan was sitting on the cot and smiled a welcome to Etta. After she had introduced him to Marius, he fluently addressed Marius—to Etta's great surprise—in the tongue of the Romans.

Marius' astonishment matched hers, but he quickly entered into a long conversation with Lathan, and after a while nodded to Etta. "His mind is very clear, indeed," he smiled, "and from what I understand, he has some friends in high places in Rome. I hope that Aurelius will be willing to send a messenger for him." He rose quickly and left the tent. Etta stared at Lathan.

After Freder had found Lathan half frozen in the woods, Etta had nursed him back to health. When she had heard from Freder that Lathan was a druid priest, she had felt awe and a little fear. She did not know much about the rites and practices of the druids, but, like many of her kind, stood in awe of the powers that people ascribed to them. Her own beliefs were simple ones. She had joined the other women in the village in their rituals in spring and summer to make sacrifices to the Goddess by the sacred spring. She had had little use for the stories of magic and powers of other gods and spirits. Here now had been a man who belonged to those who wielded real power, and Etta did not know how to deal with him. But over time, she had found him to be not only a man of great wisdom and a generous heart, but also one who had much knowledge of people and faraway places. And his deep knowledge of nature had added much to Etta's store of healing skills that she had learned from her father's sister.

She had enjoyed his tales of other countries and people, but they had had little more reality to her than the tales of gods and magic creatures, which the villagers would tell each other in the winter around their fire. Now it came to her suddenly that Lathan had indeed seen and done all the things he had talked about, and this new knowledge made him a new and very different person in Etta's eyes.

She saw Lathan look at her. "No, Etta," he smiled, "I am still Lathan and your friend, even though I speak foreign languages and know people in high places."

Etta blushed, and then sighed with relief. "Lathan," she said "if they set you free, will you be able to send a messenger back to the village and let them know what has befallen us?"

Lathan's face became serious. "Let us hope that Aurelius will hear me and send a messenger to my friends," he said. "It will be a while before either of us can hope for freedom."

It was a full five months that Etta and Lathan spent in the barracks of the soldiers, in the garrison town at the river's estuary, before a messenger came to Lathan with a sealed letter to him and one to Aurelius. The winter had been unusually hard, and travel through the lands on the continent had been difficult and the traverse over the Alps impossible until the snows melted.

Etta, together with the other women, had been told to help with work in the large kitchens. The soldiers had harassed none of the women. But shortly after they had begun to settle in their daily work routine, which got them up at daybreak and kept them on their feet till dusk, Etta saw both Kara and Nell take up liaisons with one or the other of the soldiers. At first Etta felt angry and ashamed, but then she realized that these two women had little hope of being let go to return to their village and so were making the best of their situation.

She spent whatever little free time she had with Lathan, who had been housed in the officer's quarters and, perhaps in anticipation of the confirmation of Lathan's connections in Rome, was treated more as an equal than a prisoner. He spent much of their time together teaching her the rudiments of the Roman language and told her about their gods and culture.

"They are a powerful people, Etta, and their empire will reign over the countries on the mainland for several generations. But it is their need for power that in the end will bring them to fight among themselves, weaken their power, and thereby bring about their own destruction."

A few times Etta had asked Lathan about his own life prior to coming to her village. He told her a little about his childhood in a mountain village in the northern parts of the Alps and his early wanderings after his village had been burnt by the Roman army. An officer had taken the boy on as a personal servant and, liking him, had him educated with his own sons in his house in Rome.

He had allowed Lathan to leave his service when he became a youth, and Lathan had traveled widely and studied with philosophers and physicians in Greece and Persia. He had traveled to the northern countries to study the rites and ceremonies of the druids and had been on his way back to Rome when a winter storm had found him unprepared in the mountains north of her village.

It was a mild spring evening with the sun setting in the hillsides in the west when the courier arrived with the letters from Rome. Etta was sitting in Lathan's room, resting her aching feet and listening to him playing an old song on a small harp that Marius had found for him.

After a brief knock, Aurelius entered. He looked at Lathan and, after clearing his throat, which Etta suddenly realized covered embarrassment, addressed Lathan with a formality that Etta had never heard from him before. Her knowledge of the Roman language was still slight, but she understood that Lathan's friend had indeed confirmed his identity and requested that he be set free and assisted in every way to come to Rome.

Lathan acknowledged Aurelius' message with the same formality and courtesy, and then addressed him with a request, which Etta suddenly realized pertained to her own future.

Aurelius appeared doubtful in the beginning, but at some point in the conversation appeared to assent to whatever request Lathan was making. He rose from the chair, saluted Lathan, gave Etta a courteous nod and left the room.

Lathan stepped to the window. All day the spring winds had been blowing strongly over the hill on which the barracks were built. The buds on the birch trees at the bottom of the hillside had just begun to open their tender green leaves, and their sweet smell was filling the room. The moon, nearly full, dipped in and out between high-flying silver clouds.

"We are free, Etta," he said quietly, but his voice carried such joy that Etta's own heart filled with it.

"Where do we go now?" she asked softly. "Will we be able to go back to the village now?"

Lathan's face seemed to be hidden by shadows like the moon outside the window. "Etta," he said, "little friend, there is no more village. I had a messenger sent through Marius months ago. He found the village burnt down and no sign of anybody having been there since the winter. The women must have left before the winter snows to seek shelter in other villages. The messenger went through some of the nearby villages, but no one could or would tell him if they had heard or known anything about the people in your village."

Etta stared at him in disbelief. She had, through all these months, held on to the hope that some day she would be able to go home. And now there was nowhere to go. For a long time she stared with burning eyes into the night, her heart aching with emptiness.

Lathan laid his hand gently on her arm. "You can come with me, Etta," he said. "I have already bargained for your freedom with Aurelius. He will let us go on a ship that will take us to Rome in a few weeks. You will find the country very different from this one, but it is full of beauty and sunlight and flowers. I think you will like it. And you will find new friends there, I promise you."

"How can I leave my son and Freder's mother and go to another country so far away that I may never return?" She turned to him in disbelief. "How can you expect me to do this?"

"Etta, nothing happens without the will of the gods. They have taken from you what you thought was your birthright as a woman—a good man, a healthy child, and a safe home. They are now offering you new gifts—an opportunity to learn about a new people, gather new knowledge to add to your healing skills, and find new friends. You have the chance to create a new life filled with a richness you cannot yet imagine. But you have to be willing to take the risk and let go of the past."

Etta shivered in the night wind that blew up the hillside. "Lathan," she whispered, "did the gods take these things from me as a punishment?"

"Oh, Etta, life offers us change as a chance for learning—to begin to understand that nothing in life is forever: people we love, things we own, our bodies. Accepting change sets us free so we can

know our true, timeless being—the spirit that creates our bodies
and uses it to learn, day after day, life after life. If we cling to the
things that are temporary, then we begin think that they are all
there is, and we will never know the freedom of the spirit."

Etta sat deep in thought, looking out into the moonlit valley.
If she was not Freder's wife, not the daughter of her father, not the
mother of her child—who then was she? And with a sudden lifting
of her heart, she saw that she was free to be and learn and love—
without limits, without conditions.

"I will come with you," she said, and Lathan turned to her
from the window where he had been watching the clouds pass
over the moon.

"It will be good to travel with you, little friend," he said joyfully,
and the spring moon emerging from the clouds bathed his face in
silver light.

On the day before their departure, Aurelius, looking ill at ease,
came to Lathan and asked to speak to him alone. It was a long time
before he left Lathan's quarters, looking relieved and acknowledging
Etta, who had just returned from some small errands for their
journey, with a smile much more friendly than his usual perfunctory
nod.

Etta entered Lathan's room. He sat by the window, looking
out over the river shimmering below the hillside in the warm spring
sun. "What did he want from you?" Etta asked anxiously.

Lathan turned. "He wanted to ask a favor," he said. "He cares
more than he dares to admit as an officer in the Roman army. He
asked me to take Phillipus home with us. He has been quite ill of
late and can no longer fulfill his function as an officer. Aurelius
does not want him to come to shame while on duty, so he is sending
him back."

"What ails Phillipus?" Etta had seen little of Phillipus since
their arrival in the barracks. But whenever she had met him by
chance, he had greeted her kindly, and when her growing skill in

the Latin language allowed her to speak with him, he had always inquired into her well being. She had never forgotten his look of compassion when he had told her of Freder's death.

Lathan sighed, "He has been drinking for many months to forget what he was ordered to do in a country far away from here. They sent him this far north, hoping it would help him to forget, but his memories are following him and hounding him, even in his dreams."

"What was he asked to do that he cannot forget?"

"He was ordered to execute every man, woman, and child in a village where a Roman soldier was killed—murdered by rebels. The villagers had nothing to do with it, but the commanding officer was going to make an example, and although Phillipus tried to argue with him, he had to either follow the order or be executed for treason. He was a well-trained Roman officer. He did what he was ordered to do. Now he is killing himself trying to forget."

Etta shivered. It came to her how easily this could have happened to her village. And though she had no knowledge of the whereabouts of Meta and her child, she could continue to hope that they had found shelter and that they were alive and well.

The sea journey on the merchant ship was pleasant. Although Etta had never been on a ship or seen the open ocean, she loved the wide horizon and felt no discomfort at the rolling motion of the ship.

Phillipus, who had joined them on the ship, appeared tired and ill, his past sturdy strength diminished. He stayed below deck during much of the journey. On several nights Etta woke up to hear him crying out as if in terror in the cabin he and Lathan were sharing. Then she would hear Lathan speak to him in his calm voice, and the screaming would stop.

The winds were favorable, and after debarking in a harbor full of noise and people and strange smells, Lathan was met by the servants of his friend. They traveled quickly on horseback from the dankness and turmoil of the harbor to a large white villa outside of Rome, surrounded with tall, dark cypress trees and cool courtyards, where a marble fountain spouted silver streams of water from the mouth of strange fishlike creatures, which Lathan told her were called dolphins.

Etta was bewildered and a little frightened. But Lathan's friends, Petronius, a tall silver haired man, and Livia, his much younger, cheerfully plump wife who reminded Etta with sudden longing of Meta, were kind. After greeting Lathan with great joy, they served them with delicacies Etta had never seen or tasted. Later, a little servant girl took Etta to a room that bewildered her in its strangeness. It had a floor covered with pictures laid in tiny flat stones—flowers and birds and strange wild animals. The servant girl led Etta to a bed that stood on thin legs, covered with cool linens so finely woven that Etta wondered how this could be done. But she was so tired and overwhelmed by all the new things that she had seen that she fell into a deep sleep.

That night Etta had a dream. She stood again in the doorway of her house in the village looking into the fog. She knew she was waiting, but this time she was not afraid. Suddenly the fog began to lift, and the sun began to break through the haze. Three figures came toward her in this golden glow, and as they came closer, she saw that they were Freder, Meta, and Phillipus. Lathan, who stood beside her, laid his hand on her shoulder.

"These are your companions, Etta," he said. "They have been with you before and will be with you again. Love them as I love them and care for them. There will be others."

In the morning, Etta could remember little of the dream, and she felt shy to speak of it to Lathan, who spent much of the day in serious conversation with his Roman friend.

Phillipus was weak and remained in his room most of the days.

Three weeks after their arrival, Lathan came to Etta, who was sitting with Phillipus on a shady terrace. The villa was overlooking a hillside sloping steeply to the ocean shimmering below them in colors Etta had never seen before.

Phillipus had weakened steadily since their arrival, and his initial plans to return to the home of his family further down the coast had been repeatedly postponed. His face had taken on a dusky color, and there were times when he was so weak and tired that he had to be carried to and from the terrace by the servants.

Lathan looked at him with compassion. He sat beside him and took his hand. "I will have to leave for a while, my friend," he said. "I have to go on a journey that may take a few weeks or several months, and we may not see each other again in this life. But I will see to it that you are well cared for."

Phillipus looked at him with a faint smile. "You have been good to me, my friend," he said "and you have given me back my peace. What more could I possibly ask of you?"

Etta looked at Lathan. "What do you want me do to?" she asked, her voice trembling. "Will you come back, and if not, where shall I go in this strange country?"

Lathan smiled. "Etta, little friend," he said, "don't be afraid. You will stay with my friends as long as you want. I have sent word to Marius and have asked him to come and join us. Only this I ask of you for now—stay with Phillipus. His body will not battle much longer, but it would set my mind at rest to know that you were with him until the end. My journey will bring me back to you again, be certain of that. But I do not know how soon. Use the time well. There is much here for you to learn."

He rose and Etta stood up beside him. He held her in a light embrace, for the first time since she had known him, and she marveled how tall he was. Her head barely reached his shoulders. Then he stepped back and took her face into his slender cool hands. "Take care of him, Etta." He kissed her lightly. "I will be with you again."

*   *   *

"Welcome home, Etta," the angel said, and his aura enveloped her in an embrace of pure love. "It has been quite a journey!"

Etta smiled. "It has been a good life," she said, and leaned back against the rim of a lovely fountain, its water dancing brightly in the golden glow surrounding them. She had just finished retelling the earlier years of her life journey, with all its tumultuous events and changes.

"Tell me what happened to you in your later years," the angel asked.

Etta looked at him in surprise. "Don't you know?"

"I know, but I want to hear from you what it is you experienced and learned."

Etta closed her eyes and her face lit up in joyous remembrance.

"I stayed with Livia and her husband for several years. I learned more about healing and herbal crafts from a young physician who lived close by and who worked with people in the villages near by. I helped bring many children into the world; this was always a special joy!"

"What about Lathan? Did he return?"

"Yes, he came back, and we had some wonderful years together. We had a child, a boy, and Lathan loved him deeply and taught him many of the things he knew. Then he went away again on another journey, to Egypt, to study the mysteries they teach there, and from that journey he did not return. I heard later that he died of a fever; he had given a letter and some gold to a man who was there with him, but it took many months until I knew for certain what had befallen him. I had had many troubled dreams about him but could never be certain. A few years later, I married Marius, who had come to join us and who had always been a good friend, and we had two more children. We had many good years together, and I was sad to have to leave him, but my body was tired and no longer willing to fight when the fevers came this summer."

"He is missing you very much", the angel said gently, "but he takes much consolation and strength from the children and their children."

"I am glad," Etta smiled. "I was very grateful for his love and care, and although he knew how deeply I loved Lathan and how bitterly I missed him, he never resented it, and he loved Lathan's son as much as our own children."

They sat in companionable silence for a while.

"What happens now?" Etta turned to look at the angel. "Where do I go from here? Are there other lives for me to live, as some people say, or is there a place where we will all dwell forever and ever, as others say?"

The angel smiled. "Actually, both are right, Etta. Part of you always dwells in one place, which some people call Heaven and others call Nirvana—each culture creating an image filled with their own hopes and longings, yet reflecting an aspect of truth. But your true self again and again sends forth an aspect of itself to take on a form and find an environment that allows you to gather new learning."

"How do I choose what form to take and where to go?" Etta inquired.

"Have you ever seen the light of the sun shining on a drop of water or into a shaped crystal and seen how many colors come from the one?" Etta nodded.

"So it is with the light of your soul. In order for it to experience the fullness of life, it will take on a variety of colors or qualities that allow it to experience very different things and to develop these qualities to greater perfection. For example, in this recent life, much of your time was spent in learning about healing. In another life, you may be a warrior like Phillippus, and your experience will be very different. You may be an artist or a searcher for the laws of nature, become a ruler of men or a teacher of knowledge. You will spend some lives as a merchant, learning the value and power of money and the wisdom of using it for good. You will spend some lives as a woman, others as a man, giving you very different experiences and an appreciation for the responsibilities and opportunities that each life presents. In some lives, you will be wealthy and live a life of privilege; in others, you will experience great poverty and deprivation. Each life will provide opportunities and challenges; all will result in learning. In each life, you may create imbalance and debts owed to others or you may redeem them. Your soul knows what you have mastered already and what you still need to learn."

The angel smiled again, and the light of his being shone brighter. "It will soon be time for you to shed the form you made for yourself in this lifetime, Etta, and release your name. Tell me, what was the most important lesson you learned in this life."

Etta was silent for a small eternity, while the stars circled in the timeless spheres and the colors of the heavens played and shifted around her. "I had to leave so much behind, embrace so many new situations, be a new person again and again, and yet I found that through it all, there was always a center in me that never changed, an essential me that all the outer changes could never touch. Lathan taught me to listen to that part of me when I got scared or confused; he said it was the real me, my soul."

The angel nodded. "What is the essential quality of this real you?" he asked.

Etta again thought for a while. "Loving others," she said softly, and the angel's face bent toward her with a radiant smile.

"And that is the essence that you will take with you; for in all you have done and experienced, it is this that made you truly who you are."

He reached out his hand and Etta rose up to him.

"Where do we go now?" she asked as the angel moved along the path of the light shining before them.

"You will soon see," the angel laughed, and as they moved upward, she felt lighter and lighter, as if she were rising through shimmering water up into the sun.

CHAPTER TWO

The Flight

The girl woke up with a start. Sitting for hours in the cab of the small truck and staring at the dark road emerging under the yellow beam of the headlights had finally put her to sleep. Her grandmother, her arm still protectively curved around her, was still sleeping, her head falling back a little against the hard backseat of the truck. The girl turned and studied the profile of the young driver who sat slouched in his seat, holding the steering wheel steady with his right arm, a glowing cigarette dangling from his lips.

She wondered how her mother and sister were doing, sitting on the furniture in the back of the open truck, with only ropes to hold on to and covered with all the blankets they owned to warm them against the cold damp November night.

The truck had driven up to their house as soon as it was completely dark that night, and the driver had pulled into the backyard to shield it from the view of the neighbors. They had quickly brought their belongings into the yard, and then the driver and a friend of her mother's had loaded the two beds, the table, and the four chairs onto the truck and stacked their boxes and trunks between them. The truck was so small that even this small load was piled high and the driver had shaken his head.

"I don't know that it will be safe for you and your daughter to sit up there, Lady," he had said.

But her mother had been firm. "We all have to go tonight," she had said. "There will soon be no more roads open to get us across the border. You yourself have said so." And so they had tied ropes across the truck and around the legs of the table and chairs and the bedsteads.

When they finally found Mushi, their black and white cat, and tried to put her into the laundry basket that was to be her traveling place, the cat had fought and cried so much, that the driver finally protested: "How do you think we will get across the border with that cat making such a racket?"

And so the children, with tears running down their faces, had given the cat to Grandma, their father's mother, who had chosen to stay behind. She had not been able to bear the thought of abandoning the old house where she had borne and raised her only son. She had said that she was too old to start all over again, even though she knew they could live without fear in the western part of the country. She also knew that this would be their last chance to get across the border, which with each day became more and more fortified and dangerous to cross. The town, with its medieval narrow streets, the half-timbered houses, the old cathedral, and the castle towering over the red-shingled roofs, had been her home all her life. "I am an old woman and they won't bother me," she had said, and she was left standing there holding the cat, her beautiful white hair framing her lined face like a lace shawl.

The girl tried to shift her body a little without waking her grandmother, and the driver, noticing that she was awake, turned to her.

"Hi," he said, "awake, little girl?"

She sat up stiffly. She was nine years old and not a little girl anymore. But she only nodded and continued to stare at the road. Tall poplars stood on both side of the road, their straight trunks shining silver in the headlights of the truck and their branches raised like arms in prayer, reaching up into the dark. "It looks like a cathedral," the girl thought. "We are driving in an endless cathedral." And the thought consoled her, thinking about the cathedral at Christmas, with all the candles flickering in the dark and the images of Mary and Joseph and the Christ child glowing on the stained glass screen by the altar.

When she leaned toward the window on her grandmother's side, she could see the stars. She thought she could see Orion and blue Sirius under it. Her father, the last time he had been home during the war, had taken her outside one night and shown her how to find Orion.

"It is like a big butterfly," he had said. "The three stars in one line are the body, and it has beautiful large wings. And the blue star below it is the flower it has been looking for." After that, she had always been able to find Orion when it was in the sky.

The driver was sitting up straight, scanning the road before them. He turned off the main headlights and the road in front of them glowed dimly with the two small yellow lights. He drove very slowly now, and suddenly the truck lurched and shook, and he stopped it, cursing. "The bastards have plowed up the road," he said grimly, "and done God knows what else to it. We have to go through the fields."

He started the truck again. The engine coughed, sputtered, and died, leaving the heavy smell of gasoline in the air. The driver cursed under his breath and tried to start the motor again. This time it just growled and died. He got out of the cab and lifted the hood. The girl could feel her heart beating hard in her chest.

Her grandmother whispered, "What is the matter?"

"I don't know," the girl whispered back. "I think we are at the border and they ripped up the road. But now the truck won't start."

The driver came back to the cab, rummaging in an old metal box under his seat, and went back to the hood. The girl could hear her mother's voice asking a question, but she could not understand the driver's answer. In a few minutes, he climbed back into the truck, and seeing the anxious faces of the girl and the old woman, he tried to smile reassuringly. "Just flooded," he said, and the girl had an image of a great wave that had come up from the road and engulfed the motor. The truck started up obediently this time, and the driver turned it slowly into the ditch, which separated the road from the fields on both sides. It leaned heavily to one side, and the girl thought with worry about her mother and sister in the back. They drove very slowly over a field full of wheat stubble, and then back into the ditch and onto the road. The driver suddenly turned the headlights on again and forced the truck into high speed, so that the girl was pressed back into the seat.

They drove this way for a few minutes, the old truck rattling and shaking, and after turning into a bend sheltered on both sides by huge old fir trees, the driver stopped and turned off the ignition. He climbed out of the truck and lit a cigarette, and the girl saw that his hands were shaking so badly that he needed two matches to light it. He went to the back of the truck and said to her mother, "Well, Lady, we made it. We will be in the next village in ten minutes."

After this, they drove more slowly, and suddenly the girl saw through the right window that the dark night sky was beginning to pale. They were driving on a broader road through open fields again, and she saw that the fields were filled with people, people walking slowly with burdens on their backs, or people sitting on chairs in the middle of the field. It was a strange sight, these silent shadows moving over the empty fields, and the girl tugged at the driver's sleeve. She pointed wordlessly at the people, and the driver cast a glance at her and then at the moving figures. He seemed to understand that she was frightened.

"Only people, who walked over the border with their stuff," he said, "waiting to be picked up by friends or family. It's all right," he said reassuringly. And the girl sighed and curled up by her grandmother's side and fell asleep. She woke up when she was lifted out of the truck by a big man with a friendly face, who handed her to her mother. She could see the lines of exhaustion from a night spent in fear and cold on her mother's face, but also a smile and a joy in her eyes, which she could not remember having seen there for a long while.

They carried her up the stairs in an old farmhouse, which smelled of a freshly started fire and baked bread, and tucked her into a bed still warm and smelling of sweat, but she quickly fell asleep while the sun rose brilliantly in the window . . . .

*   *   *

Italy, circa 100 AD

Claudia awoke slowly out of a long dream. The dream had been pleasant—she had been sitting in her garden watching the fountain shimmer in the sun, and Petronius, her gardener, had brought her a gift from a friend, a large cage full of beautiful small birds, their feathers shining with all the colors of the rainbow. She had sat and listened to the birds twitter and talk among themselves. But then the birds had fallen silent and would not sing anymore, and Petronius, who worked by the fountain, had come at her call and looked at the birds.

"They are birds used to freedom, Domina," he had said. "They will not sing in cages."

So Claudia had opened the cage and the birds had flown free, but they had all settled in the bushes and trees in her garden and had started to sing again, while the sun glittered in the rising spray of the fountain. It had been a very peaceful dream, and she did not like having to leave it.

She leaned forward on her arm, watching the moonlight flood the tiles on the floor with a sharp blue light. The light seemed to make ripples on the mosaic, and the water around the dolphins playing in the waves seemed to move. The house was very quiet, and the only sound she could hear was the wind whispering through the old gnarled olive trees on the hill below the house.

She stood up and wrapped a light cloak around her shoulders. She felt suddenly hungry and decided to go down into the kitchen to find some small cakes to eat and wine to warm her.

She opened her door softly, so as not to wake the little slave girl sleeping on her pallet in the corner. The arched passageway was well lit by the moonlight, paling the oil lamps on the walls. In the courtyard, the fountain was murmuring softly to itself and the smell of roses was heavy in the air. As she turned the corner of the courtyard, she saw a shadow step forward from the passage leading to the servant quarters, and Mara, her housekeeper, came up to her. Mara had been in her service since they had both been young girls, and had been Claudia's personal servant and confidante for many years. She had risen in trust and responsibility and now ran most of the household and supervised the women servants so independently that Claudia had to spend little time and energy on these matters.

Mara, her dark hair beginning to streak with gray, her body heavy from the birth of five children, laid her hand on Claudia's arm. "Are you ill, Domina?" she asked, concern showing in her face.

Claudia smiled. "No, Mara," she said, "just restless and hungry. But come and help me find my way around in the kitchen. It has been a while since I came to beg some sweetmeats from cook." Both women smiled in memory of the old cook who had always scolded and muttered and yet had always let them have some candied fruit or sweet cakes.

As the two women walked slowly towards the kitchen, which lay in total darkness, Claudia turned to Mara. "And what are you doing up in the middle of the night?"

Mara was silent, and for a moment Claudia had the feeling that she was searching for an answer. Then the moment passed, and Mara turned to her with a smile. "Keeping my servant girls in order," she said. "The young Tyrenean slave that came to us this spring, she has taken a fancy to the stable master, and I found her hiding in the stables trying to be invisible. I sent her to her quarters but wanted to make sure she stayed there." Claudia studied Mara's profile in the light of the kitchen fire that the older woman was rekindling. It was not like Mara to concern herself with the nightly doings of slaves. But Claudia trusted her old friend to have her own reason for this explanation and so held her peace.

The next morning rose cool and clear, and Claudia woke early and refreshed. She remembered her nightly excursion with a smile and, after a brief bath, went to feed her birds, which were kept in large cages and brought out into the garden during the day. She had just begun to open one cage to fill the food bowl with fresh seeds when the porter came through the garden at as nearly a run as his considerable paunch would let him.

"Domina," he gasped, "Domina, an Imperial officer and guards are at the gate demanding entrance to search the house."

Claudia stared at him in disbelief. "Search the house for what?" she asked irritated. "Don't they know that this is the house of Senator Marcus Tribenius? Even though my husband is dead these five years, Rome surely owes him and his widow some respect and some rights."

"Oh, Domina, I told him so, but he just stood there and said he had orders to search every house on the road to Perusia for escaped Christians."

"Escaped Christians?" Claudia frowned. "Why in Jupiter's name would I hide Christians in my house? Bring the officer to me. I am sure this is a misunderstanding."

She picked up her cloak and, patting her hair into place, went to sit on a small marble bench in the shadow of a tall oleander bush.

The porter quickly returned with a young man, tall with a face deeply tanned by the sun and eyes curiously light blue in the dark face. He bowed perfunctorily and introduced himself: "Valerius Pausanius, captain of the Imperial guard, sent to follow and recapture a group a Christians imprisoned in Rome last week and sentenced to die in the arena for conspiring against the Emperor. We know that they came this way, for we followed the tracks of two carts. This morning we found the abandoned carts outside the village down there. They cannot have gone far on foot, and we suspect that they have found shelter here."

Claudia sighed and rose to her feet. She was not a tall woman, and years and childbirth had turned the slenderness of her girlhood into a matronly figure that gave her stateliness.

"Captain, I left Rome five years ago after the death of my husband to find peace and consolation in this house far away from the troubles and intrigues of Rome. Now you come to intrude and disturb my peace. I can assure you that there are no hidden Christians in my house. I have never set eye on anyone of that strange sect, and my household and I are servants of the gods, as are you. You will find all the proper shrines in their assigned places, and the people in the village will testify that my household and I perform all the sacrifices as the priests decree them. But if your duty forces you to intrude into the peace of my household, I have no men at arms to stop you. Go and search the house and the grounds with your men, but pray do not let your men trample all over my flowers and disturb my birds. I cannot speak for my gardener's temper."

The officer smiled, bowed briefly and returned shortly with a troop of twelve guards, who spent the next hours searching the house from cellar to roof, combing the gardens and fields surrounding the villa, and then spreading out into the small village nestling at the foot of the hill below the house. It was late afternoon when they finally returned to the road, hot and disgruntled, mounted their horses, and rode back on the road toward Rome.

Claudia tried to ignore the disruption of her household and spent the afternoon embroidering a tunic for her youngest granddaughter with a beautiful gold thread. Mara fussed all day after the guards, scolding them when they broke a wine jar and generally made a nuisance of herself. Again Claudia wondered at this, for Mara was usually a calm and well-controlled person. Petronius, her gardener and Mara's husband, continued to plant some new trees and calmly directed the two young boys who were helping him with the heavier garden chores, and completely ignored the searching guards.

The sun had sunk behind the hills in the west and the sky was paling into gentle shades of pink and lavender when Mara approached Claudia. "Domina, I need to speak to you in private," she said softly, and Claudia wondered at the troubled expression in the older woman's face. Claudia rose, stiff from sitting so long in the now cool evening air.

Mara walked in front of Claudia, moving swiftly for a woman her age and figure and, to Claudia's astonishment, led her out of the garden through the little side gate down the steps to the foot of the hill. Claudia stopped at the bottom of the stairs and asked sternly, "Mara, where are you taking me?"

"Please, Domina, it is important. Please trust me." And Mara hurried on through the growing dusk past the houses of the village.

It was only when she turned off the road leading out of the village to Perusia that Claudia realized that they were approaching the hill that sheltered the old cave that had served past generations as a temple.

Mara moved quickly on the goat path winding through the low shrubs and high grasses at the bottom of the hill. They came to the wooden door that the villagers used to close off the old temple, which now served as a stable for the village goats in cold weather. Mara stood for a moment listening at the door and then knocked twice, waited, and knocked three times again. The women waited for what seemed like a long time. Then the sound of a drawn bolt could be heard, and the door opened slowly. Claudia held her breath. She did not know what she expected to see behind these doors. She was not prepared to see the picture that presented itself to her eyes.

The old cave temple, long abandoned, its walls black with the smoke of the fires of the goatherders, was aglow with the light of tallow candles. The old stone altar, too heavy to be moved, was covered with a white cloth embroidered with gold. But what shocked Claudia most was the sight of a group of children, twelve or more, the youngest barely able to walk, the oldest nearly a young woman, who all sat quietly huddled on the ground, staring with serious eyes at the women.

Mara moved into the cave, and drew Claudia in behind her. "Quickly," she said, "We have to close the door, so that the light will not be seen."

At that moment, a man entered from behind a curtain covering the entrance to another smaller room carved out of the rock. He was of slight build and not very tall. His brown hair was longer than the usual Roman short-cropped style, and he had eyes dark like the eyes of a fawn that Claudia had once seen in the gardens of a woman friend in Rome.

He approached the two women and bowed courteously to Claudia, and then bent quickly down to Mara and kissed her. "The Lord bless you, Mara," he said quietly, "for your courage and your love of these children."

Claudia turned to Mara. "Are these the people the guards were searching for?" she asked incredulously. "Are these children Christians?"

Mara looked at her, searching her face as if to read her mind. Then bowing her head, she said, "Yes, Domina, these are children of Christian parents. The guards took them when their parents were imprisoned. Some of the guards in the prisons are Christians themselves, though secretly, and they were able to take the children from the prisons and bring them out of the city at night."

"But what is your part in all this, Mara? Have you then taken on the belief of these people, too?"

Mara lifted her head and looked at Claudia. Some expression in her eyes touched Claudia deeply. She could not find a name for it, but she remembered her late husband looking at her this way the day she had borne his first son.

"Domina, I wish there was time for you to learn more about Him, the Christ, who brought the new teaching to this world so that people could know the power and mercy of God's love. But right now, we have to find a way to take these children to safety. There is a small village in the mountains north of here where some Christians have found shelter. Only a few people know the way. Lucius here and Petronius are two of them. Tomorrow, they will take the children hidden in oxcarts to that village. You could help us by sending Petronius on the road to Perusia to bring back stones from the quarry for your gardens. This way, his absence will not arouse suspicion." She peered anxiously at her mistress' face.

Claudia suddenly felt tired. She sat down heavily on a small stool and stared at the children. The children sat quietly, returning her glance. The youngest, a little boy with curly brown hair toddled over and smiled up at her. He searched her face as if looking for familiar features, and slowly his smile turned into a frown and then into an expression of such desolation that Claudia's heart ached. She picked the child up and held him close. "Who will take care of these children?" she asked Mara.

"We hope to free more adults and take them to the village. There are already five, though two were badly hurt when they escaped and may not live."

Claudia stood up. She set the child down and turned to Lucius. "I will send Petronius with food and drink for these children tonight and enough for the journey. Will you come with me now and speak to me about this new teaching that has aroused so much feeling in so many people and that has made my own servants keep secrets from me?"

She turned to Mara. "Stay with the children now," she said firmly. "They are in need of a mother, and you have more experience with that than I do." She smiled and Mara sighed with relief.

Lucius followed her back to the house through the dark and silent village. Only some dogs barked as they passed the houses, the old stone walls white in the moonlight.

In the room, which had served her husband as a study, she bade Lucius sit. She had noticed that he was limping when they climbed the hillside steps and asked him if he too had been injured in the escape.

He shook his head, "No, Domina, not this time," he said. "This is an old injury from a time when a mob attacked a friend of mine." His face clouded in the memory and his eyes darkened.

"Also a Christian?" Claudia inquired gently.

"We had no name for ourselves then, but yes, we followed the teachings of Jesus of Nazareth, who is the Christ."

"Did you know him yourself, this man they call the Christ?"

Lucius smiled. "No, Domina, He lived and died before my birth."

"What, then, is it about this man that makes people follow his teachings after He is dead for years?"

"He taught that only by loving, not only those dear to us, but also those who hate us, will there ever be peace on earth and we will become free from our own fears and hates and needs."

"But how can a person learn to do that?" Claudia stared at Lucius in disbelief.

"He showed us through his own life." Lucius' voice was very quiet and the wind whispered in the leaves of the bushes outside the window. The flame from the small oil lamp trembled and cast dancing shadows on his face. "He could have been king and have earthly power. There were those who offered Him wealth and this kind of power. He chose to love the poor and outcasts; He healed the sick and the blind, and in the end, He forgave his enemies and died for his beliefs. He could have saved Himself but He died consenting. They say He rose from his grave after three days and was seen by his disciples and others, and continued to teach them for many months after."

His face was very still and his hands rested quietly in his lap. But Claudia could feel a strength in him that belied his slim figure and mild countenance. "Do you believe this? You seem like a man with learning. Do you believe someone can come back from the dead after three days?"

Lucius smiled slowly, "Domina, I am a physician, and I was trained to believe in what I can see and touch and smell. But I have seen the healing of people that all my experience told me could not be healed. And it was done in His Name. I do not know whether He returned from his grave in his body or in his spirit. He often spoke to those traveling with him, saying that man had to be born twice, once by woman in his earthly body and once by his soul into a body of the spirit. There are old teachings of the Greek philosophers who speak of this same body of the spirit, and I believe that Jesus lived in this body of the spirit like you and I live in our physical bodies. Yet He brought something that none of the old teachings taught before, and that is this new law of love that is the very essence of God, the Creator of Life. I believe his spirit is alive in those who follow this teaching of brotherly love and even in those who have never heard his name, yet love their enemies."

Claudia sat in thought for a long time. Lucius sat with her in silence, sharing the small evening meal a servant had put before them. He ate and drank sparingly and after a while rose, thanking Claudia for the meal.

"I need to return to the children," he said. "Mara will be tired. She bathed many of them last night and dressed the wounds of those hurt in the escape. She had little sleep, and she is not young any longer."

Claudia had to smile. So here was the explanation for Mara's wanderings last night. Errant servant girls, indeed.

Just as Lucius turned to go, Petronius entered into the study.

He was breathing heavily and his words came hard. "A messenger came from Antonius. Somebody has betrayed us to the guards. I have word that they will be back in the morning, and they know now where to look for the children."

"We will need to move them tonight then," Lucius said firmly. "Can you help us with provisions and the use of your oxcarts, Domina?" His brown eyes were searching hers. "I know that the belief of these children's parents is not yours and that helping them may put your safety and wealth in jeopardy. But will you consider helping us simply because they are only children?"

"If they know where to find the children, won't they also know where you were planning to take them?"

"Lord Christ have mercy," Petronius stared at Lucius. "Where will we take them now, and who will warn the others?"

"Wait," Claudia's mind was searching quickly. "There is an old stone house in a small valley in the mountains to the west. It belonged to my husband's father, and nobody has used it in many years. It is very isolated and there is no road to it now, just a goat path. But is has a spring and there are woods close by. We could take the children there until the guards have given up the search."

"But how will we find it if nobody has gone there in many years and there is no road to follow?" Petronius shook his head in despair.

Claudia felt Lucius' eyes on her face. "I have to go and warn the others," he said quietly. "Mara and Petronius will need help. Will you go with them and the children and show them the way, Domina?"

Claudia thought of her home, her peaceful life, her gardens with their richness of flowers and exotic birds. She thought of the cool fountain in the courtyard and the long gentle afternoons spent in leisurely conversation with friends.

And then she thought of the children, homeless, without parents, hunted to be brought back to die. And she remembered her dream: how Petronius had brought her a whole flock of new birds that would only sing in freedom.

She smiled. "I will go with the children and take them to the house. Petronius can come back and leave you instructions how to find us when you return."

Lucius took her hands and lifted them to his lips. "I will find you and the children wherever you are. And we will find more time to speak of the Christ and his new law of love."

The rising sun found Claudia sitting beside Petronius on the front seat of the old oxcart. She was dressed in Mara's old clothes. Mara was sitting with one of the older girls on a second cart following close behind. The children had left the temple in the middle of the night and had been guided through the sleeping village to Mara's small house adjacent to the villa. Petronius and Lucius had worked feverishly to load the carts with provisions and to lead the reluctant oxen from their stables behind the house, all the while trying to explain to the roused servants why the lady of the house had taken a sudden fancy to travel to Perusia to buy stones and plants for her gardens.

After the cart had traveled some distance from the villa, the children had joined them and had hidden in the straw under old blankets. They had driven the oxen hard in the beginning, trying to cover as much distance under the cover of the night as possible. After the moon had set, only the light of a small lamp dangling from the lead cart had shown them the rutted road. The night air was cold and Claudia shivered in the thin and worn clothes, thinking of the children sleeping the sleep of exhaustion under the blankets they had hastily gathered from the storage rooms in the villa.

Some of the children had started to cry when they had been told that they had to leave again, but the older ones had taken the younger ones by their hands and had spoken to them quietly, and the weeping had stopped. Now all of them were asleep, and only the oldest one, the girl nearly old enough to be a woman, had remained awake, sitting upright in the cart staring into the night sky.

Lucius had ridden with them part of the way and at the first sign of dawn had once more said goodbye to Petronius and the two women. Their eyes had followed his slight figure for a long time as he rode up the steep path leading into the mountains, sitting easily on a small roan mare.

Claudia was worried. She knew that they would not have the slightest chance of escape if the guards encountered them on the road, and she prayed to the spirit of the man she had heard named Jesus the Christ to protect her charges who were persecuted in his name.

Three hours after sunrise, she found the narrow stone path leading away from the main road into the mountains. They followed it for a while and stopped the carts in a small cypress grove that gave some shelter and shade from the sun already beating down from a brilliant sky. In the center of the grove lay some fallen pillars, and some patches of mosaic on the ground showed the outline of an old small temple. A thin runnel of water emerged from a tumble of rocks at the foot of the rising mountains. The children, stiff from crouching in the carts, climbed down and thirstily drank the ice-cold mountain water. It was very still in the grove, and the only sounds were those of the crickets and the trill of a lark invisibly singing high in the silvery blue sky.

Claudia sat down in the shade of a tall cypress tree, leaned against a flat bolder, and closed her eyes. The excitement of the last night had worn off, and she was weary. Mara and Petronius were talking with the children in low voices, and Claudia slowly slipped into a light sleep.

The sudden sound of horses riding up the narrow rocky path to the grove had the children scrambling back into the carts, fear clearly written in their faces.

Valerius, riding in front, reined his horse, a big brown stallion, close to Claudia's cart. "Traveling, Domina?" he said courteously, "But, surely, this is not the road to Perusia. Have you lost your way?"

Claudia could feel the heat rising in her face, and suddenly she felt a great anger in her heart at this arrogant young Roman with his mocking face. But she kept hearing Lucius' calm voice in her study. "Only if we love those who hate us will there be peace in the world."

And suddenly her anger left her like the wind blows away the smoke of a quenched fire and she saw the young officer with new eyes. She could feel his frustration with a task he hated, his concern with his own career, which would rise or fall with his willingness to follow orders, no matter how meaningless or cruel.

"Valerius Pausanius," she addressed him with a gentle smile. "You searched my house and grounds all day yesterday and found nothing. Won't you let me and my servants travel in peace today? We are on our way to find new plants and flowers for my gardens. There are some beautiful wild flowers in those hills, and I long to bring them back to my gardens for my friends to enjoy."

The officer looked at her steadily, searching her face. She held his glance for a long while, and her heart was filled with love for the children she was protecting and pity for this young man forced to pursue a duty he despised.

He lowered his eyes, glancing casually at the blankets in the oxcart behind Claudia. She dared not follow his eyes for fear that her concern would betray her.

"Domina," he said, and there was a new look in his eyes, as he returned her smile. "Take good care of the flowers in your gardens. I do not think that the Emperor could be interested in the small wild flowers you are likely to find in those arid hills. Someday, when I am not on duty, I would like to see how those wild ones you are searching for today are prospering."

And with a slight bow, he rode back to the guards who were waiting on their horses like statues in the shadows of the cypress trees.

Petronius snapped the whip at the oxen that started their plodding steps up the path, and Claudia felt the wind drying the tears on her face.

A hawk circled high above them, his fierce cry filled with the joy of freedom.

* * *

Claudia looked at the angel in surprise. "So there is a Heaven and angels as the Christians are teaching," she said, "I have always wondered about that."

The angel laughed, and his laugh was like the silver bells that had chimed in Claudia's rose garden so many years ago. "There were Heaven and angels eons before there ever were Christians," he said. "All true religions have known and spoken of this. But the Christians, as young as their history is, already feel that that they own the only truth, and that will be a great difficulty for them and others for a long time to come."

Claudia looked at the angel in astonishment. "But did not the Christ say He was the Son of the Father in Heaven, and is that not so?"

The angel nodded. "Truly it is so," he agreed. "But there have been others before Him and there will be others after Him who will reach the same level of awareness that He had reached, which let Him speak of Himself as the Son of the Father. He Himself said to his disciples that they and others would do even greater things than He. He said he was a light on the path, an example of what humankind can become if it follows him on the path of love."

"Love," Claudia mused. "It always comes down to love, doesn't it? Lucius always talked of love as the heart of his teaching, and it has always been love that made it possible for me to do the things that appeared impossible."

The angel smiled and his radiance increased. "Yes," he said, "you have loved much, and through it you have served many. Tell me, what happened to the children you rescued from the soldiers?"

"We kept them in secret for a while in the house in the mountains, and slowly, over many months, found safe homes for them with families who were Christians themselves or just kind human beings who felt children deserved love and care no matter what their parents believed. I returned home after a while and continued to help Lucius guide other Christians to safe places when the persecutions became worse in Rome."

"Putting yourself at risk even though you never became a Christian yourself?" the angel wondered.

"I loved the things Lucius told me about the Christ and what He taught, but I found that I did not like many of the things His followers preached; some of it seemed so narrow and not at all filled with the love they were proclaiming. And there was so much talk about sin that they could no longer enjoy life and love and all the good things the gods give us. I just cannot believe that that was what their teacher meant."

"No," the angel said sadly, "there truly was too much talk about sin, and not enough about joy, and He was always full of joy. And this will darken their path greatly as they move forward in history."

Claudia looked up at the angel in wonder. "Will they survive the persecutions, then, after all?"

"Oh yes," the angel said," they will not only survive the persecutions, but will grow strong and become a dominant power in the world for many centuries to come. They will bring some change for the good but also much evil, forgetting the essence of the law of love and becoming greedy for power and material things. They will persecute others even more cruelly than they were ever persecuted themselves. And their responsibility will be greater because they were given the new law of love and yet they will disregard it."

"But," he continued, "let us not mar the joy of your return with the problems of their future, dear friend. You have done well this life, and you have given much and have never hesitated to risk all to serve others. That is all that matters in any life."

Claudia chuckled. "You mean I will be allowed into Heaven even though I was never baptized by the Christians?"

"Child," the angel's laugh joined her as they passed along

beautiful gardens full of roses more magnificent than any Claudia had ever grown in her own, "it would be a very empty Heaven indeed if only baptized Christians were allowed here! It would have been empty for eons, and we angels would have been bored for eternity waiting for a few Christian souls to arrive. The heavens and the levels below it are open to all souls as they pass through on their way to their next life, and according to their actions and their level of awareness, they will take the high roads or linger on the lower ones for a while."

"Are there next lives for all of us?" Claudia asked in wonderment. "Some few of the Christians spoke about this, but many scoffed at them and denied this as a possibility."

"Christ Himself spoke of it, but it was not the focus of his teaching this time," the angel said. "Yes, it is the path of learning for all souls, Christians and others alike. How else could souls gather enough experiences to learn the fullness of God's creation and their own divine potential?"

"I have often wondered about that," Claudia said, "especially when I saw how very different people's lives were, some very rich, some desperately poor, some always in good health, some crippled from birth, or when children died so very young as many do. How could there be lawfulness or justice in that?"

"All souls come from God and are on their road to return to God, and each life is a small step towards the completion of their divinity."

"Even a life filled with hate and darkness?"

"You need to experience all the possibilities that human beings are capable of, and then make choices. Some lessons are learned only in darkness," the angel said quietly, and there was a shadow in his face that made Claudia feel cold.

"Will I, too, have to live a life in darkness?" she wondered aloud.

"You already have, and you learned much from it," the angel replied.

"What could I possibly have learned from such a life," Claudia exclaimed, "and why do I not remember it?"

"Your soul remembers the lesson you learned, and it was a lesson about the absence of love. You have learned that lesson well, as your most recent life has shown so clearly. The details do not matter and would not help you if you recalled them again. But let us leave these past things behind. There are old friends for you to meet and new places for you to go," and with that the angel grasped Claudia's hand and lifted her up so that they suddenly floated over the gardens. And there on a hillside, in the shadow of tall cypress trees, to Claudia's great delight, were her husband, and Mara, and Petronius, and all the other friends who had died before her, smiling and greeting her. And with laughter and joy they gathered around her to show her the delights of the spheres where they all would dwell for a while before embarking on another adventure and another life together.

CHAPTER THREE

The Monastery

The young woman looked up the narrow street leading to the top of the hill. The old stone pavement was worn from centuries of people climbing up and down the hillside. The houses to either side of the street were old, with stone walls rising to red tiled roofs, the high narrow windows filled with flowering plants. Vines reaching up from gnarled old stems spread out as if suddenly let free into the bright sunlight. The sun had passed noon a while ago, and Ethan had found a small restaurant with an outside garden where they sat under shade trees and enjoyed a light lunch of bread and cheese and red wine.

"Monk's food," he joked and she wondered if monks were allowed wine other than during mass. "Oh yes," he answered, "in the past, it was part of their daily fare, but it was mixed with water—not so much as to make the wine less strong as to make the water safe to drink."

They had come to Florence three days before and had spent much of their time wandering about in the old city, visiting monasteries now turned into museums, admiring marble domes and churches, and sipping cappuccino in ancient squares with views of famous old buildings. They had chosen to stay in a small pensione, which offered few modern conveniences but had a huge bedroom with beautiful old white and blue floor tiles, and was furnished with a large bed with a carved oak headboard, two straight-backed chairs, and a sturdy old oak table. The room was so big that the furniture seemed a little lost in it. In the afternoon, with the wooden shutters closed, the sun crept in through the slats, making magical patterns on the floor, lighting up the golden halos of the Virgin Mary and St. Francis on the walls.

Ethan had told her of the years he had spent studying in Florence and of his wandering through the hills of Tuscany, visiting and spending some time in the monasteries in the hills. This landscape seemed so much more the home of his soul than the Scandinavian country where he had spent his childhood years.

She could feel it in the joy with which he pointed to the tall, proud cypress trees standing guard beside the old villas on the hillsides, the love with which he showed her details in the frescos of Fra Angelico, the pleasure with which he took her into narrow backstreets to find a memorial plaque that told of the birth of a famous sculptor or painter of the Renaissance.

It would be easy to imagine him in the brocades and silks of a Florentine patrician, she thought, studying his face as they walked up the narrow street. They came to the top of the hillside and he led her to a low stone wall that opened up to a view of Florence in the valley below. Gnarled old olive trees covered the hillside, their silver-green leaves shimmering in the afternoon heat. She and Ethan sat for a while on the wall, watching the water of the river glisten in the sun.

"Come," he said, "I have more to show you." He took her

hand, leading her up broad stone stairs to an open courtyard. The walls of an old monastery surrounded it on three sides, while the fourth opened to a view into a garden with pathways disappearing under shady trees. "This whole hill was part of an Etruscan City." Ethan pointed, "Below this garden is an old amphitheater, and the monastery was built on top of old Etruscan ruins."

They entered the small church, dark after the bright sunshine outside and smelling of frankincense. They sat in a pew, watching the flickering light of the Eternal Lamp. A monk entered from a small door by the side of the altar, his brown robe hiding the thinness of his old body. He genuflected in front of the altar and then turned, peering into the church. He saw them and approached, softly asking them questions in Italian, which she did not understand. Ethan replied, and the two engaged in a brief exchange until she suddenly heard the old man say something that was unmistakably in a Scandinavian language. Ethan laughed and turned to her.

"Father Umberto here was a sailor before he became a monk, and he spent years on a Danish ship. Then he went as a missionary to China, and now he has come back to his monastery to spend his last years teaching the novices."

The old monk smiled, his bright blue eyes young in a face with skin like old parchment.

"He says there are beautiful Chinese ivories in their museum, gifts from rich Chinese families to their missionaries, and well worth seeing," Ethan continued. The monk nodded and addressed Ethan again. "He says that they don't have a guide today, but as there are no other tourists, we can go around on our own. They are using only part of the monastery now and have changed some of it into a museum open to the public. There are fewer novices each year, he says."

Father Umberto smiled again and bowed a little, pointing the way to a door in the side of the chapel. They thanked him and entered through the door into a little hallway leading to a wide stone arch. A tall iron gate barred the entrance to a cloistered garden filled with summer flowers dreaming in the sun. She could hear the songs of several birds, the chirping of sparrows, the humming of bees busy among the flowers, and the splashing of the fountain in the middle of the garden. She stood very still, pressed against the gate, looking into the garden. She felt tears running over her face and was filled with the pain of an ancient sorrow. She had lost all sense of time when she felt Ethan's arm around her shoulder. "Come, little friend," he said gently. "You cannot hide here again this time."

He smiled at her and turned her from the gate. "Let's go and look at those Chinese ivories instead . . . ."

*   *   *

Italy, circa 1300 AD

Francisco stood at the top of the hillside, gazing at the city below. He thought he could see the roof of his father's house on the east side of the dome, but the sun was in his eyes, and the heat haze made the air shimmer and flow like water. He thought with sadness of the heated argument he and his father had had that morning. In the end, the old man had risen from the table, slamming his fist down so hard that some plates had jumped off the table. His face had been red under the bushy gray brows, and his fierce blue eyes had glared at Francisco.

"Is there no way I can make you see that there are more important things in life for my son than a pretty face and a sweet smile and soft hands? Will you let this little romance ruin years of friendship with Elena's family? Do you have any idea what will happen if I have to tell Giovanni that you refuse to marry his daughter?"

Franciso had glared at his father with equal temper. "Father, it is not just a little romance. I love Angela, and Elena would be very unhappy if I married her with the thought of another woman in my heart at all times."

The old man had turned on his way to the door: "Love, my son, is much more than sweet feelings in the moonlight and songs sung under your lady's window at sunset. But it does no good to talk to you now. Go and speak to Julian up in the monastery. Maybe he can get some sense into your besotted head."

With that he had stomped out, slamming the door behind him. Francisco's little sister, Lucia, had sat in the corner wide-eyed, listening to the exchange, and afterwards had come up to him, taking his hand into her two small white ones.

"He will be not so angry in a little while. Just wait, brother," she had whispered, and Francisco had had to smile at the womanly wisdom in one so young.

He had taken his chestnut mare and ridden up the winding road to the monastery, thinking of the change that had come into his life these past six months. It had been last December, during the Christmas season, that Elena's cousin Angela had come to visit. Francisco had met her during one of his weekly visits to Elena's family. The slight, dark-haired girl with the warm brown eyes and the gentle voice had been so very different from tall and stately Elena, with her dark blonde hair always neatly laid in tight braids around her head, with dark brows over cool gray eyes that seemed to look straight into your heart.

It had taken only a few visits before Francisco had found himself completely enchanted by Angela's sweet temperament and gentle ways. Elena had sat silently, embroidering elaborate patterns on a pillow, watching the two laugh and play chess and sing together, with Francisco playing the lute.

Francisco sighed deeply. He turned and slowly climbed the broad steps leading up to the monastery. He hoped that Julian had received his message and would have time to talk to him after the noon mass. He missed the friend of his childhood. Julian had come to live with his family at the age of four, after both his parents, close friends of Francisco's father, had died of the summer fever in the same year. The boys, close in age, had spent their first seventeen years together, had been tutored by the same teachers, and had learned their martial skills from the same sword master.

One day, three years before, Julian had come to his foster father and told him that he would go on a pilgrimage. He had left town the following day, without a horse or servant in spite of his foster father's urging, and nobody heard anything from him for six months. When he returned, grown thinner, silent, and tanned from weeks spent walking in the burning summer sun, he had told his foster father that God had called upon him in his dreams to become His servant and that he would join the Franciscan Brothers to succor the poor and sick.

Francisco had been deeply shaken by Julian's sudden decision and tried to argue with him. But Julian had only smiled at his arguments, and his deep-set gray eyes had taken that far away look that had so often frustrated Francisco in the past. "We have different destinies, little brother," he had said, and his smile had seemed to come from the same far distance as his gaze. "God is asking different things from us. May we both serve him well."

Francisco entered the little chapel. It was cool and dark and peaceful. The noon mass was over, but a few old women from the village still knelt in prayer, and the silence was deep.

He waited in the chapel for a little while before Julian entered from the side door, recognizing his friend in the back of the chapel and approaching him with a quick energetic step.

"Becoming a monk has not slowed you down much," Francisco whispered.

Julian laughed softly. His lean face had become even more ascetic in the past three years, and the tonsured hair had changed his outer appearance even further. Yet the warmth of his smile and the liveliness of his clear gray eyes were those of the old friend, and Francisco felt fleeing from his heart an anxiety that he had not known was there.

Julian took his hands. "What brings you here with such an urgency, little brother?" he asked, peering into Francisco's face as if to read the answer there.

"I need your advice and your clear head." Francisco's distress showed clearly in his eyes. "My father will not listen to me and I have no one else I can trust to help me understand my own feelings and make the right decision."

"Come then." Julian turned and led him through a side door out of the chapel. "There is a peaceful place where we can sit and talk for a while and not disturb the prayers of others." They walked through an arched hallway that led into a cloistered garden filled with summer flowers. Julian drew Francisco to a stone bench. "Let us enjoy the sun before the shadows bring the cold to these stones," he laughed. "Now tell me what is troubling you, my friend."

Francisco leaned back against the stone wall that radiated the heat of the sun. He let his eyes rest on the peaceful garden in front of him. "Maybe I should leave all my troubles behind me and become a monk too," he sighed.

Julian chuckled. "I am not sure you have quite the temperament for the monastic life, my friend. But before you make such a serious decision, do tell what has so upset the joy you usually take in the beautiful things of life."

Francisco turned and sighed, his dark eyes troubled. "It is about Elena."

"Has something happened to Elena?" Julian inquired, his eyes seriously searching Francisco's face.

"No, Elena is well. Something has happened to me. Last winter her cousin, Angela, came to stay with her for the Christmas season, and we fell in love. I have told my father that I cannot marry Elena now. It would not be kind to her, and I cannot bear the thought of living without Angela."

Julian looked at Francisco for a long time. "How long have you known this girl?"

Francisco sighed. "She only stayed for a month. Then we sent letters to one another and I have gone to visit her twice since. She

feels the same about me as I do about her, but she also feels guilty
because she loves Elena and does not want to hurt her. But we just
cannot live without one another. I have spoken to her father about
marriage. He is a silk merchant and would be pleased to let his
daughter marry me, given my father's position and business in
Florence. But he knows that Elena and I have been pledged to one
another by our families since childhood, and he will not give his
permission until Elena's family has released me of my father's
promise."

"And Elena?"

Francisco avoided Julian's searching eyes and looked at his hands
clenched in his lap. "She has not said anything. She looks pale and
becomes thinner every day and spends much of her time in prayer
in her room. I wish she would be angry at me and shout and throw
things like my little sister does when she is furious with me."

"She is not a little girl but a grown woman who sees her father's
hopes for her and the continuity of his family in danger."

"Are you then also against me and my love, even you who I
thought knew me and loved me?" Francisco's voice was pleading.

Julian smiled though his eyes remained serious. "No, I am not
against you, my friend. I only wanted to show you how Elena
must feel in this situation. Have you spoken to her yourself?"

"How could I, with her looking so much like a martyred saint
and everybody making me feel like Judas? Besides, I do care for
her, but more like I care for Lucia. I have never loved her. I know
that now. What I feel for Angela is something I have never felt
before. And it is not only the lust of the flesh, either," he added
quickly. "I have known that and know it for its passing pleasure."

"Yes, I guess you do," Julian said, and although his face was
serious, his eyes twinkled. He remembered well his friend's
escapades that never led to anything but a fast quenching of an
urgent physical need and no lasting commitments. This time a
deeper feeling seemed to have taken hold of his heart.

Francisco turned his troubled face to his friend. His eyes
brimmed with tears. "Do you, too, think I am just filled with

foolish notions, as my father tells me every day? I love Angela deeply, yet I feel anguish for the hurt that my love must inflict on Elena and on our families, who have been so close for all the years of our childhood. But I know if I follow my father's wishes, we all will be unhappy for the rest of our lives. I would come to resent her and even hate her for taking my happiness from me."

Julian sat in silence and gazed out over the flowering garden where the fountain splashed in the sunlight and the bees hummed in the lavender bordering the beds of summer flowers. Then he turned to Francisco. "Speak with Elena. She has known you for a long time and loves you well. Tell her what you feel about Angela and what you feel about her."

"But what if she won't release me from my father's promise?" Francisco searched his friend's face who was smiling at him reassuringly.

"Trust me. Talk to Elena."

Francisco rose from the stone bench. "I trust you more than any other person in this world, my brother." He bent down to embrace Julian. "I miss you and your friendship."

"That you always have, no matter where you are or what you do," Julian held him close for a moment, and then also rose. "Come back and tell me how your talk with Elena went." With that he turned and entered a small wooden door leading from the cloister to the brothers' cells.

Elena was quiet and kind and understanding when Francisco revealed his heart to her. She told him that she had seen his love to Angela grow and did not want to stand in their way. She had talked to her father, calming his outburst and had dried her mother's tears over her daughter's misfortune. Three weeks later she entered the Order of the Holy Claires.

Julian only smiled when Francisco rode up to the monastery to tell him the essence of his conversation with Elena.

"Did you know that Elena would choose to become a nun?"

Julian nodded. "She always longed to enter the religious life. But she was a good daughter first, and her father's wish to join his house to your father's was not to be denied. And she liked you well enough that the idea of becoming your wife was not completely distasteful to her."

"The thought to be my wife distasteful?" Francisco stared at him in disbelief. "You are surely joking."

Julian laughed. "At the risk of hurting your vanity, my handsome and charming friend, but even life with you cannot compare to life lived for the glory of God."

Francisco returned to his father's house, bewildered and at a loss. It seemed that there were things about Julian and Elena he had never perceived before, and it troubled him. But then the joy of soon being joined with Angela drove all such thoughts from his mind.

Francisco and Angela were married in a small private ceremony on a glorious September day in the small chapel of the monastery. Both Francisco and Angela had wished to abstain from a grand wedding feast to spare the feelings of Elena and her family.

Their first child was born at the end of June of the following year, a pretty little girl they named Marcia. The child thrived, and Francisco was spellbound by the miracle of her growth. Angela teased him and told him that he had more eyes for his daughter than for her. Even Francisco's father mellowed under the smiles of his granddaughter, and he finally made his peace with his son's choice of wife.

A year passed, and Francisco watched in joy and wonderment how his wife and daughter blossomed, and his happiness was complete.

In the spring of the following year, Francisco decided to join Angela's father, Pietro, on a trip to the northern provinces to establish new outlets for their silk business. Angela was four months pregnant with their second child and Francisco felt there was sufficient time to complete his business and be home again before the birth of the new child.

Francisco's sister Lucia was entering her twelfth year and had begun to show the same beauty her mother had been admired for before death in childbirth had taken her from her family.

On the morning of the departure, Lucia, Angela and the child joined the men in the courtyard to say goodbye to the travelers. Marcia, wiggling on her mother's arm, pleaded to sit on her father's horse. Her little warm fists gripped Francisco's fingers tightly as he guided the horse twice around the courtyard, and her big brown eyes shone with excitement at this new experience. He lifted her from the horse, ignoring her protests, and carried the firm, warm little body back to her mother, who raised her high up and then held her close.

"Wave goodbye," she whispered. "Papa will be gone traveling for a while. He will bring us back some beautiful things if you are good."

Francisco embraced them both and kissed Angela. "May the Lord watch over you and guard all of you," he smiled, and laid his hand gently on her swelling body. "I will be back well in time before this little one will join us."

Pietro, a tall broad shouldered man, graying at the temples but still young looking, laughed. "If you don't tear yourself away now, we will never get on the road, and the child will be born before you get back."

Francisco lifted himself into the saddle. The morning sun slanted over the tiled roof into the courtyard and shimmered on the rising waters of the fountain, transforming it into a pillar of gold. The light surrounded the women and the child with a radiant glow, and Francisco thought of a painting of the Holy Family he had seen in the house of one of his father's friends. His heart was filled with a joy that ran golden like the light in the fountain, and he said a brief prayer of thanks for the blessings that had come to him in the past three years.

It was on their journey home two months later that they received the first news of an outbreak of the Black Death. Brought into the country by sailors on a ship moored in Venice, it had spread quickly through traveling merchants, and people were falling prey to it in several of the northern towns. Francisco and Pietro and their train of servants rode in haste on smaller roads, trying to avoid towns and villages and to reach Florence before the illness struck there too.

They rode into the narrow streets of Fiesole at sunset on a hot July evening, only to be met by the sound of bells tolling ceaselessly through the clear evening air and to find their way obstructed by processions of carts piled high with bodies, drawn by men garbed in black robes, faces covered with cloth to keep the stench and the flies away.

The two men sat on their horses, staring. "Let us find Julian," Francisco whispered hoarsely. "He can tell us how long the illness has ravaged here and in the town below." They rode wearily to the monastery, sometimes turning their horses aside from bodies fallen in the street. Pietro's servants rode behind them, whispering among themselves, their faces stricken with fear.

Francisco rang the bell at the monastery gate, but nobody came to answer. He pushed the door and found it open. The hallways were dark and only the refectory was lit with smoking oil lamps. Five monks were tending rows of people stretched out on straw on the bare ground, and the moaning and crying of the sick and dying and the stench of the illness nearly overwhelmed Francisco.

One of the monks, kneeling beside a sick woman, wiping her brow with a moist cloth, looked up as he came closer.

"I am looking for Brother Julian," Francisco whispered, afraid to raise his voice in this house of death. The monk stared at him, his face drawn by exhaustion, empty of understanding. "Brother Julian," Francisco repeated louder, desperate. "Is he alive?"

A light touch on his shoulder made him wheel around. Julian stood behind him, a Julian terribly changed, his eyes sunk in deep hollows, his face lined and aged.

"Julian, what happened to you," Francisco's voice broke. "Are you also ill?"

"I was, but I recovered before the illness came on us in full force. I had tended the earliest victims and became one of them. They say if you survive it once, it has no power over you again. So now I can tend all my brothers who cared for me."

"What is happening in the town below? Has the illness taken its toll there as much as here?"

Julian looked at him with sudden realization. "You have not been home yet?" There was a sorrow in his eyes that took Francisco's heart and squeezed it so that he could not breathe.

"What happened in my home?" he whispered, and a cold sweat broke out over his body. "Please, tell me what happened."

Julian's eyes were filled with compassion. He took Francisco's shoulders and held him close. "Your sister lives," he said softly. "She, too, was ill, but she lives. I cared for her myself. Angela and Marcia were dying when one of your servants came to call for my help. There was nothing anyone could do for them. Your father died three days after them. I think the grief speeded his death."

Francisco stared at him. A sob broke from the depth of his heart, and he clung to Julian's thin shoulders. "No, oh my Lord, no, you cannot do this to me. Oh my Lord, have mercy on me."

Julian held him close until his sobbing abated a little. "Come, my friend, rest in one of our rooms. There is nothing more that can be done now. Lucia is safely with Elena in St. Claire's nunnery. There is nothing you have to do tonight. Stay and rest with me."

"Pietro, he is waiting for me outside. I have to tell Pietro."

"Let me tell him," Julian said firmly, and led him to a small cell, bare except for a narrow straw-covered pallet, a prayer stool, and a small writing desk. "Rest here until I return. I will bring you wine and bread, and then we can talk."

Francisco sank down on the straw. He did not move until Julian returned, carrying a pitcher with red wine, a loaf of stale brown bread, and a lit candle.

He sat down beside Francisco and slowly broke pieces of the bread and fed him like a child. He made him drink most of the wine and, in the end, Francisco fell asleep in his arms, crying like a child in his mother's lap.

For two months Francisco stayed with Julian, spending his days tending the monastery's vegetable gardens, herding the goats on the hillsides, and bringing food and milk to the monastery. Julian asked him to stay away from the sick and dying, and told him that he could be more helpful by taking care of the tasks the brothers had tended to in the past. More than half of the monks had succumbed to the disease, and those remaining were exhausted from weeks of caring for the sick and the dying in the village and for those who had sought refuge in the monastery.

Sometimes Francisco wondered if Julian wanted to spare him the sight of the victims suffering from the plague or wanted him removed from the disease to save him from contracting it himself. Much of the time, he did not care one way or the other, but worked from sunrise to sunset to numb his mind and his body, to fall into an exhausted, dreamless sleep each evening.

In September, with the cooling of the days and nights, the plague subsided and the number of newly ill and dying decreased sharply. People reappeared in the streets, and so did the first signs of commerce. Julian and Francisco rode with Pietro into the town on a cool, rainy morning. The cypress trees stood tall and silent on the hillsides like dark angels weeping over the devastation they had watched in the past months.

The large house by the dome, his home, was cold, dank, and empty. Those servants who had not succumbed to the disease had fled the town and gone back to their families in the country, where the plague had not struck as severely as in the crowded city.

An old guardsman had stayed behind with his two dogs to protect the house from looters. They found his remains in the cellar. He had set the dogs free before he became too ill to take care of them. The house had been looted of all movable possessions, its furniture, and art.

Francisco wandered through the house like a stranger. He barely remembered the splendor of the rooms with their painted ceilings, glowing chandeliers, rich tapestries, carved wooden chairs and tables, paintings and marble statues.

He could not feel anything, nor could he think of what to do next. All his life, the house had been alive with the warmth and love of his mother, the vitality of his father, the laughter of his sister, the life and movement of servants, of guests and friends. Then it had been filled with the radiant joy of his love for Angela and, later, the sound of Marcia's little voice. He thought of the unborn child whose face he would never know.

In the end, he turned to Julian, who had walked with him through the house. "I cannot stay here. There is nothing here for me to do. Let me stay with you at the monastery. I can tend your gardens and your goats. I have learned at least that much these past weeks."

Julian looked at him with serious eyes. He had regained some of his old energy and strength. "There is much for you to do, my friend," he said compassionately. "You have a sister to care for, and Pietro will need all the help you can give him with his business. When things return to normal, there is your father's business and his fortunes to be administered, and the city will have need of your skills and money to recover from this devastation."

Francisco shook his head. "I cannot do it any longer," he said bitterly. "There is no reason for me to go on. Let Pietro manage his own business. He did well enough without me before. In a year or two, I will find a good husband for Lucia, who will be glad of a large dowry. I will turn my father's fortunes over to the church. My uncle, the bishop, will know how to use it best for the welfare of the poor and the sick. Let me go in peace. I cannot carry these burdens any longer. Without Angela and my father, there is no reason for me to go on."

Julian frowned. "What do you intend to do, then, if not to fulfill your responsibilities to your family and your city?"

"Let me serve God as you do." Francisco stared out of the window into the empty courtyard where the silent fountain reminded him of the last joyful morning of his departure "Let me enter your monastery and serve God."

"Running away from life is not a way to serve God," Julian's voice was sharp. Francisco turned and stared at him.

"But you chose to do it. Living your life for the glory of God is the most important choice one can make, you always said."

Julian looked at him and his voice softened. "Little brother, God called me to render a service to him. My time in the monastery is only a preparation. His Church is in desperate need of change if it shall live and serve His will. Brother Francis showed us the true way of living the Life of Christ, but the old patterns were already too strong. His life was a living example of Christ's teaching. Yet he did not live within the structure of the Church to affect its power directly. Already there are those who have broken away in righteous despair because the true teaching has been corrupted and betrayed by the greed for power and material things. There will have to be changes wrought in the very heart of the Church to bring back His true spirit. Soon I will have to leave my peaceful monastery and take on the burdens of power and deal with those who will use power for their own ends. It was not to escape responsibility that I entered the monastery but to take it on as God called me to do."

Francisco stared at him in astonishment. Never before had Julian spoken to him of his vocation in this way. Never had Francisco understood clearly why he who had always been the brighter student, the more skilled orator and brilliant philosopher, should have sought the quietude of a monastery to live out his life in anonymity.

Then he lowered his head again into his hands. "You have your calling and your path, my friend. I envy you for your sense of purpose. I have lost mine, and I cannot see a new one anymore. Let me come with you and help you in your task, or let me go to a place where I may find some peace of heart and mind."

Julian bent down and took his friend's face into his hands. "Listen to me, little brother. Please listen to me. You are still in the darkness of despair. Do not make a decision now. Take some time, travel, take your sister home with you. You will see—there is life and love and joy waiting for you. But you have to risk living and loving again."

"Can't you see?" Francisco cried out. "That is exactly what I dare not do again. I loved so much; I was so happy. And now it is all gone—all the love, all the life. Let me go in peace."

Julian shook his head sadly. "We do not find peace by denying our destiny, no matter how hard it seems. But if you cannot find the strength in yourself now, go, and may you find the peace you are looking for." He turned to go. Then he stepped back and touched Francisco's shoulder. "Our paths may not cross again for a long time. But some day I will come back and teach you to dare to love again." There was a deep smile in his eyes as he bent down to make the sign of the cross over Francisco's head. The empty rooms echoed the sounds of his steps, and the autumn rain ran like tears over the small windowpanes.

*   *   *

The angel looked at Francisco and shook his head. "Well, what did you learn this time, I wonder, my friend?"

Francisco looked around him in surprise. "This is not what I expected," he exclaimed. "Should I not be in purgatory?"

"And what do you expect purgatory to look like?" the angel wondered.

"A place where I have to suffer for my sins, as the Church teaches," Francisco replied.

"Well, the Church does not know everything, and besides, the idea of purgatory pays them well in donations from all the people afraid to be punished for their sins. It is a handy idea," and the angel laughed at Francisco's dismayed look. "But yes, as people have created strong habits or passions, they will carry that energy with them even after death and will live with it until it slowly dissipates over time. What sins do you suppose you have committed that you should suffer for?"

"I pursued many young women in lust when I was young, and even when I was a monk, my blood grew warm when I saw a beautiful young woman passing by!"

"Well," said the angel, "I never did think you would make a very good monk, because that was not really your task for this life. Your so-called sins this life were much more sins of omission rather than commission."

"What do you mean by that?" Francisco exclaimed.

"When you entered the monastery, you abandoned the responsibilities that should have been part of your learning for this life. Your burdens fell on others: your father-in-law, your former bride, and your sister. Julian tried to tell you this again and again, but you were feeling so sorry for yourself, you did not want to see this."

"But I withdrew to the monastery because I loved Angela and Marcia so much, I could not live without them."

"You lived quite well without them, for five more decades. You just avoided caring for others who were also your responsibility," the angel said, and his voice was very dry.

"Does it not count that I became a servant of God?' Francisco asked meekly.

"And how exactly did you serve God hiding away in a monastery, I wonder?" asked the angel. "Do you think the only way to serve God is praying seven times a day and not acting on your lustful thoughts? Might you not have served him better by using the talents you were given, by using the money that was yours for the good of others, by being a power for good in the town you were born?"

"Will I be punished for this then?" Francisco asked, and in his heart he wondered what punishment he would receive.

"Oh, for heaven sake, grow up," the angel exclaimed. "Have you learned nothing yet in all these lives? It is not a question of punishment; it is a question of taking responsibility. In this life, you avoided taking on the responsibilities that were yours, so this becomes an outstanding debt. You were trained as a merchant, were you not? You owe this debt, so you will have to balance it out. You create your next lives by what you do or avoid doing in this one, and the people to whom you owe a debt will became part of your fate in the future."

"So God is not angry with me for my sins?"

"Francisco, listen carefully," the angel said and he sounded a little tired. "God has nothing to do with the problems you create for yourself. You were given free will, and it is up to you how fast or slow you learn. You can choose to correct the imbalance you have created in one life or over many lives. The most important thing for humankind to learn is that this universe was created by love. God **is** love, and when we truly act out of love, we do God's will. It is really quite simple."

There was a long silence and the angel waited, gazing at Francisco, who finally raised his head and looked at the angel as if seeing him for the first time.

"I don't think I ever really understood what love truly is," he said regretfully, "not in the way you talk about it. I think Julian knew, and his life was an act of love far beyond the kind of personal love I pursued."

"I am glad you can finally see this," the angel said, and for the first time, he smiled at Francisco, and a golden radiance streamed from his heart. "Make sure you remember! And now, let's go and see Julian. He is very busy and has some work for you."

"Work, here in Heaven?" Francisco exclaimed.

"Well, did you think we just sat around all eternity playing the harp? Somebody has to keep humankind from making a bigger mess than they have already. So come on, let's go," and with that, he took Francisco by the arm and hurried him along a steep path to a building reminiscent of an old Roman palace, made of translucent pink marble. They entered and found themselves in a vast round interior courtyard, where a large fountain played in the center. Many doors opened in the periphery of the space, and the angel led Francisco to one of them. They entered a large room lit by a warm golden light, although Francisco could not see its source.

The room was filled with shelves overflowing with books and scrolls. Julian, looking the way he had as a young man, was sitting behind a large table. He nodded at Francisco with a quick smile and pointed to a pile of scrolls on another table.

"Welcome back, little brother," he said. "Read those for me, and report their content to me later, will you, my friend?"

Francisco, with a happy smile, set to work.

CHAPTER FOUR

The Wave

The young woman sat in the sand, close to the curved line the last wave had made rushing upon the shore. Broken pieces of shells marked the ocean's border. With small running steps, a flock of sandpipers followed the water as it receded back into the ocean. The sun stood high in the sky and sea gulls drifted on the wind, gliding along the length of the beach. A big dark brown gull was sitting on a wooden post marking the jetty of rocks stretching far into the surf. The gull rose and, with a raw squawk, flew with heavy beating wings to the open ocean. She leaned back onto the sand and let the sun warm her. She was bone tired from long days and nights working in the hospital, and it felt good to let her thoughts drift to the far edge of the horizon. She could hear the laughing of children farther down the beach, but she had walked a while to find a quiet place, feeling a need for solitude.

It had been three months since she had arrived in New York City. There had been weeks of packing and saying goodbye to old friends and family. The eight-hour flight across the Atlantic Ocean had been filled with anticipation, and Ethan had smiled at her excitement and joy in starting a whole new phase of her life.

The city had been different than she had expected, knowing it only from movies and postcards. Ethan had shown her the fancy avenues and the deteriorated slums, the spacious parks and the grand museums. He had taken her to the mountains and lakes only an hour away from the millions of people crowding into the city every morning. Today they had driven to the beaches that stretched for miles along the Atlantic coastline.

She had at once felt at home in the city, moving among people from so many nations, and contrary to what she had heard from others, she had found many of them helpful and friendly and not at all aloof.

After years of only studying, she had received a new sense of reality from her work in the large hospital. It had been a challenge to practice medicine in a new language and a new environment, but she enjoyed the challenge and had found her colleagues willing to make allowances for occasional slips.

The warmth of the sun made her drowsy and she was drifting into sleep, soothed by the timeless rhythm of the breaking surf. A sudden shadow fell over her face and she opened her eyes. Two of Ethan's friends were bending over her, smiling. "Come on, sleepyhead; this is not the time to take a nap. You will get burnt if you lie here much longer. Come into the water with us before the tide goes out. Later, the undertow becomes too strong to swim here."

She sat up, looking out over the water, and then turned back to them and grinned. "I had such a peaceful time until you woke

me, and this water looks awfully cold on such a nice warm day."
She stood up, stretching and slapping the nearest one on the back,
and ran towards the water: "The last one in pays for dinner!"

The cold of the water took her breath away, but after a few
strokes, it felt more comfortable. She rode the incoming waves and
was soon outside the range of the high surf. She could see her
friends swimming behind her. She turned towards the eastern end
of the beach and swam parallel to the long, sandy dunes. It felt
good to stretch out, and she enjoyed the motion of the long swells
of the waves as they rose and sank slowly under her until she could
see nothing but the water all around her.

She swam until she was tired and then turned to look for her
friends. They had fallen behind and motioned her towards the
shore. She let the waves carry her closer to the beach, waiting for a
tall one to carry her in to the shore. A large swell rose up behind
her, higher than all the others, and she paddled slowly to rise to its
top. The wave kept rising and suddenly broke under her, dropping
her several feet with the full weight of the water crushing down on
her. She choked and gasped, trying to find the way up in the
turmoil of the swirling white water, and finally found some foothold
in the sand below. She tried to stand up to get some air, when the
next breaking wave knocked her down again, tumbling her
helplessly over and over and over....

*   *   *

Pacific Islands, circa 1500 AD

Taluhe sat on the beach, scratching an itch on his foot with a
broken shell. He could hear the laughing and screaming of the
children playing in the shallows of the lagoon in the other cove.
He was tired, having been out all night fishing with the other men
until dawn. The air in the sleeping hut was stifling since the
morning breeze had died down, and the flies were biting in spite
of the herbs he had rubbed onto his arms and legs.

He rose and walked slowly to the edge of the beach, where a few scraggly palms were trying to survive. He leaned against a rough trunk, savoring the sparse shadow it offered. A few seabirds were walking on the waterline, picking at shells, and he could see the dark brown sails of two boats far at the horizon. A small breeze came from the water, and he lay down on the sand, resting his head on some dry palm leaves.

He awoke. Something was tickling his face and he swatted at the disturbance. A giggle brought him wide-awake. Amantah was leaning over him, a bird feather in her hand, laughing. She had put red flowers in her hair, and several pink shell necklaces hung between her small round breasts. She leaned closer, and the tips of her breasts touched the skin of his chest.

"Will you sleep away the whole day, my friend, while the village is preparing a feast with the catch you brought back this morning?" Her eyes were teasing him as she took a blossom from her hair and caressed his face with its soft petals.

Taluhe could feel the heat in his loins rising and he took her by her arms. "Will the feast wait for us, do you think?" He pulled her down and she willingly submitted to his caresses. When he entered her, she gave a small moan and then began to follow the rhythm of his body with ever-increasing passion until they both found release.

They rested for a while, and then bathed in the shallow warm waters of the lagoon, pouring water over each other, and finally they ran laughing and splashing towards the village, the spray behind them creating tiny rainbows in the sun.

When they came to the huts in the shadow of the palm grove, the older women had finished baking the fish in the embers of the central fire, and the older children had arranged fruit and baked tubers on large palm leaves and decorated them with flowers.

The men sat in a circle drinking coconut juice from the shells and talking quietly with one another. Riothe, Taluhe's father, who was also the village's master boat builder, nodded to him as he joined the men in the circle. He saw his brother Neame step out from the sleeping hut and pour himself a drink of water. Neame had been on the other fishing boat last night, and Taluhe remembered with a smile the shouting and bragging as the two boat crews had sailed into the sheltered lagoon just before sunrise and had compared their catch.

Amantah brought him some baked fish and roasted tubers cut into small slices, and sat down behind him with the other women. He ate slowly, savoring the taste of the fish and the firm sweetness of the tubers. The men were discussing the succession of the boat builders, and his father and two of the other elders were taking each of the younger men who had reached manhood in the past season into consideration.

The building of the village boats was of great importance to these people, as their livelihood and their contact with other islands depended completely on the skill of the builders. Their importance was second only to the skill of the boat guides, who could lead the boats far into the ocean and find their way back to the island by guidance of wind, wave, sun, moon, and stars. Theirs was a knowledge that Taluhe had longed to have since he was a child, and although as the oldest son of the master boat builder, his first choice should have been to learn his father's skill, his father had relented and had allowed him to become the apprentice of Rahue, the oldest and wisest of the boat guides among the Twelve Islands, the group of islands that could be reached within a five-day journey from Taluhe's island.

Taluhe had lived and studied with Rahue for the past five years, ever since he had reached his manhood at fourteen. He had spent many moons on Rahue's boat, learning to read the signs of the waves and the currents of the ocean, the smells and sounds of the winds, learning the names of the stars and their patterns and courses as the seasons changed. He had learned to recognize the signs of the storms as they built into destroying demons in faraway heavens to come racing upon the islands, and he had come to recognize the signs of the calms that could strand a fisherman far away from any shore.

He had also come to love the freedom of the open sea, feeling closed in and crowded when he returned to visit his parents; and after the endless quiet days with Rahue on the boat, where an occasional word or signal was sufficient to communicate between them, he had found the chattering of the villagers and the closeness of people in the sleeping huts increasingly difficult to bear.

He had returned to his island this season to visit his family and to see if among the young women who had come into womanhood over the past five years there might be one who would please him. His eyes had quickly found pleasure in the gracefulness of Amantah's body and the quickness of her mind. Yet she also had the rare gift to sit quietly with him and watch the stars circle in the heavens at night. She, in turn, had been pleased to find favor in the eyes of the well-built young man who would soon become a boat guide and thus give her honor as his companion.

Both families had approved the choice of the young people, and the village was planning to help them build their own hut at the next full moon.

Taluhe rose, filled with contentment and pleasure, to walk across the open space in the center of the village to the sleeping hut. The sun was setting over the water, and the small children came running up from the beach, proudly displaying their treasures of shells and pebbles that they had found during the day.

Manana, Taluhe's mother, called for Tiu and Kome, his youngest brothers, five and seven years old, to come and get some food. They stumbled up the path to the fire, tired from a day spent running and swimming, and sank down beside their mother, breathless and filled with talk about their activities of the day.

Taluhe smiled, remembering his own boyhood and the pleasure of the days hunting fish in the lagoon and finding shells that he and Neame would bring their mother to fit together for necklaces.

Still warm from the day's sun, he entered the shady hut and sank down on his sleeping place. There was still no breeze and the air hung heavy in the enclosed space. He awoke a few hours later, hot and sweating. Something had roused him, but he did not know what. The other young men, who shared the communal space, were sleeping deeply, some snoring, some tossing restlessly in the heat.

Taluhe rose and stepped out into the night. The nearly full moon stood low on the horizon, and the stars seemed dimmed by a haze. He walked briskly through the central village space. The fire pits were dark and there were no sounds, not even the rustling of palm fronds. He left the shelter of the palm grove and followed the narrow path that led up through low bushes and gnarled trees toward the black rocks at the center of the island, where a small spring bubbled out of a rock cleft, supplying their village with drinking water. The spring had not failed the village in five generations. Twice a year, all villagers went to make offerings of fruit and flowers to the spirit of the spring and at the birth of each child, the father of the child would take a gift to the spring and return with a shell full of fresh water to pour over the newborn's body.

The setting moon gave barely enough light for Taluhe to find his way among the sharp rocks. He felt restless and walked quickly. He finally reached the top of the rise and sat on a ledge, giving him a view over the village far below in the shelter of the palm trees. The moon path shimmered on the ocean, and the night was very still.

Suddenly, Taluhe saw the setting moon being swallowed by the horizon that seemed to be rising to meet the moon. He stared, not believing his eyes. And then he heard a sound he had never heard before in his life, a sighing, rushing sound, as the water in the lagoon was drawn out beyond the coral reef that sheltered it, drawn out to meet the wall of water that was now rushing up towards the island at ever increasing speed.

Taluhe stood frozen. He did not understand what had happened to the ocean, what was happening to the water in the lagoon, and then suddenly he remembered the story that Rahue had once told his apprentices—how a long time ago, many, many seasons before his own birth, the islands had trembled as if a giant's fist had shaken them, and how the water had fled from the shore and had returned in a wave so high it had seemed to cover half the sky, and how it had rushed over the islands and drowned more than two-thirds of the people in the villages of the Twelve Islands.

Taluhe ran, ran down the path, ran and fell, got up and ran, shouting, crying as he was shouting, to wake his people to flee from their huts, to come up to the center of the island, but even as he ran, he knew that his voice did not carry far enough, that he would not reach the village in time, that his people would not escape the wall of water that now rushed toward the island.

He fell again, breathless, half-stunned from his fall, and rose again, only to see the wall of water, glistening in the starlight, meet the shore with a roar and a sound of crashing and breaking and continue to move up the island as if nothing could keep it from its path. The monstrous wave finally broke, and the waters cascaded up beyond the palm grove, carrying broken trees and pieces of wood. The water rushed up the path where Taluhe stood, unable to run, unable to move, staring at the destruction that the wave was wreaking in its path. The water rose up to his chest, knocking him over, and he finally began to swim, swim with the flow of the water until he felt ground under his feet, and the force of the water broke and began to slow and then turn and recede.

He saw that the wave had carried him nearly to the top of the rocks, above the origin of the spring, and he thought in despair that not even the sacred spring had been safe from this destruction.

The moon had sunk below the horizon and the night was completely dark. Taluhe could hear the sounds of the retreating water churning as it met the waves below. There were no other sounds, except the sighing of the wind that had come with the wave and now blew fitfully in the low bushes below the rocks.

Taluhe wanted to call out but his voice was a hoarse croak when he tried, and he knew he was afraid to hear nothing but silence responding to his call. He rose from the wet stones, slimy with the debris the wave had carried, and slowly found his way down towards the shoreline. There was no longer any path to follow, and several times he slipped and stumbled over tree trunks and other obstacles in his way.

As he neared the place where the village had been, his steps faltered. The pale light of the early dawn lighting the sky behind him showed him that only a few palm trees had survived the onslaught of the wave. Of the huts, only a few central beams stood at strange angles. There were no sounds or movement anywhere.

He walked to the village center, now cluttered with debris and mud, and saw the first bodies, caught between some posts of the sleeping hut of the young men. He stepped closer to search their faces for signs of life. Their eyes were open and staring; some had gashing wounds, and already the flies gathered on them. He moved as if in sleep, finding body after body, some within the rubble of the huts, some under trunks of overturned trees. He found the bruised body of Tiu, his youngest brother, caught under a heavy beam of the Gathering House.

He pulled the small body free, holding him in his arms, rocking him like he had seen his mother rock him when he was a child at her breast, and he began to chant the Song of Return, which the villagers sang for those who had gone to the Land of the Sunset. His voice broke again and again, and his tears made it harder for him to sing, but he sang the song to its end.

Then he carried his brother's limp body out of the ruins of the village to the part of the island where high above the waterline his people laid their dead to rest. He looked for a large shell and began to dig a shallow grave. He covered the little body with sand still wet from the flood and laid down a circle of other shells to mark the place. Then he sat beside it and stared at the ocean, blue and calm with small waves running up the littered beach, as if no huge wall of water had ever come racing through the night to destroy all that Taluhe had known and loved in the years of his life.

At the end of the first day, he made a journey to the spring and found that fresh water, though in much diminished quantity, was trickling from the rocks. He quenched his thirst and filled a coconut shell to last him till the next morning.

He sat on the rock beside the spring, watching the sun sink red and clear into the ocean. There were no clouds in the sky and no sounds except the calling of some seabirds flying along the shoreline to find their roosting place for the night.

He keenly felt the island's emptiness of human sound and movement, the absence of the smoke rising from the village fires, and realized that he was utterly alone, more alone than he had even been in the nights when Rahue had sent him sailing by himself to find his way back to the island with his newly learned skills. Then, at least, he had known that he would come back to human life and community. Now there was nothing but the island and the ocean, the sky and the wind, the sun and the stars.

He had no way of knowing if anyone had survived on any of the other islands, and he knew that even if some few had survived by chance as he had, they would be struggling to stay alive and would not come to look for survivors on other islands for a long time.

Taluhe spent three days burying the fifteen bodies he found in the village. After the first day, he no longer had the strength to drag the bodies to the burial place, but simply covered them with sand where they lay. More bodies began to wash up on the shore, most unrecognizable after several days in the water, and Taluhe was grateful. He had not found his parents' bodies nor Amantah's among those in the village and he assumed that the backflow of the great wave had carried them and the bodies of the thirty other villagers far into the ocean.

After he had finished the task of burying, Taluhe took a day's supply of fried fish and water and set off to circle the island. It was a two-day journey, but he knew he could replenish his food on any of the beaches, and the spring was the same distance from the sunrise side of the island as from the side where his village had been.

He found several more bodies on the other beaches and, after chasing away seabirds and crabs, pulled them above the waterline and covered them with sand. He also found the remnants of two of the fishing boats that had been carried by the wave over the lower part of the island and had been stranded high up on the sand. Both had sustained much damage to their side walls, and their sails were torn, but one still had an unbroken hull and main mast.

Taluhe looked the boats over carefully and for the first time since the night of the wave, he smiled. Here was some hope for him, the possibility to leave the island and find his way to one of the larger islands where some people might have noticed the tremor in time to flee to higher grounds. He was certain now that it had been the tremor that had awoken him that night, but too late to make him understand its threatening nature.

He pulled the boat into the water. It floated, though out of balance, and he began to pull it through the shallow water along the beach. He tired quickly, and he realized that he had eaten little in the past days, while working harder than he ever had in his life. He anchored the boat and, after spearing several fish in the shallows, baked them in a fire made of dry seaweed and the wood that lay now everywhere on the beach. He curled up in the sand and fell asleep quickly.

He dreamed of Amantah, her face framed with red flowers, her soft breasts pressing against him, and he awoke crying. The waning moon was high in the sky and the night wind blew cool from the ocean. He sat for a long time staring out over the water and thought of the life that he had hoped for—days and weeks spent in the endless spaces of water and sky, guiding the boats of his people, returning home to Amantah and the children she would bear him, children he would proudly present to his father and mother, children for whom he would take offerings to the sacred spring and bring its water back to them.

The moon, which would have been the sign to start building their hut, had grown full and had begun to wane unnoticed while he buried his people. And now he was here, alone with water and sky, the whole island his alone. The emptiness of the island suddenly overwhelmed him, and he hid his head under his arms and cried until he fell into an exhausted sleep.

The morning sun woke him, and with its warmth and light, he found new courage. He discovered some seabird's eggs in the upper part of the island that the wave had not reached and roasted some crabs he dug out of the sand. He journeyed to the spring and found it running more freely. Then he returned to the boat, attached a rope he had twisted together of dried grasses, and began his slow journey in the shallow water back to the place of his village.

He had to swim several times to avoid some of the coral reefs that separated cove from cove, and he promised himself that the first task he would undertake would be to make a new paddle and mend the sail.

At the end of the third day, he finally brought the boat into the cove that had served their village as a harbor. He had cut his leg deeply on some of the corals as he brought the boat into the lagoon and was bleeding as he dragged the boat up on the sand.

He slept restlessly that night in a shelter he had improvised from some of the beams left unbroken by the wave and that he had covered with dry leaves. In the morning, he was feverish and thirsty and too weak to travel to the spring for fresh water. He was able to split one of the coconuts he had found on the beaches during his journey, but the juice tasted bitter and did little to quench his thirst. He lay in fever for two days, and several times thought that his mother and Amantah sat beside him, cooling his brow and holding a shell with cool water to his lips. But each time he opened his eyes, there was no one, and his thirst burned his throat and dried his mouth until he could not swallow. In the third night, a thunderstorm broke over the island and Taluhe lay in the cool rain and drank of it as it ran over his face, and then he drank the water that had collected in his drinking shells.

In the morning, his fever was gone, and although he was weak he was hungry and he made his way to the beach to find some crabs, which he devoured raw.

The moons waxed and waned and Taluhe worked, trying to remember how the women of his village had gathered plant leaves and worked them to gain fibers to repair the sails. He tried to remember how his father had cut wood and treated it and bent it over steam to shape it.

In the heat of the noonday, he would sit in the shadow of his shelter and watch the horizons for signs of other sails, and in the cool of the early morning and at sunset, he would go to the lagoon to catch his morning and evening meals.

He grew thinner, not for lack of food, but because he found no pleasure in eating. Several times he felt so hopeless about his lack of skill in shaping enough wood to repair the boat and mending the torn sail, that he left his village and circled the island again.

After the turning of five moons, he had learned how to use plant fibers to make ropes and mend the sails. He had repaired the damaged parts of the boat with wood he had painstakingly shaped with broken shells as tools and was able with the fragile fiber ropes to raise and fasten the sails.

He knew that his work would not hold up to any heavy wind or strong waves, but he hoped that he could find his way to the other islands before the rainy season with its storms arrived to pound the beaches with endless days of downpours, high winds and high tides.

He knew with a deep certainty that his will to go on living in this aloneness on the empty island had only been sustained by the hope of repairing the boat so that he would have a chance to find other human beings. Never before had he been so aware of his need for a human voice, the touch of a hand, the laughter of a child, the song of the women as they pounded roots in the center of the village. He realized that being with others was as essential a need for him as food and water.

Taluhe spent a few days preparing supplies—his greatest supply problem being fresh water. He had found none of the wooden barrels that had served the fishers of his village as water containers, and had not found a way to shape new ones without the proper tools. Hollowed-out tree trunks had split when dry. In the end, he drilled holes into coconuts and filled them with spring water, closing the drill hole with wooden plugs, hoping that the water would stay fresh long enough to be drinkable during his journey.

He set off early before sunrise, hoping to benefit from the morning wind that blew gently from the noon side of the island. The wind filled his makeshift sail, and he was happy to see it hold the wind and begin to move the boat toward the island he hoped to reach in three days' time. There would be a current half a day's journey from his island that would increase his speed, and if he could reach it before nightfall, he could let it carry him during the night.

He found the current as the sun was beginning to sink rapidly toward the horizon. He lowered the sail and watched the movement of the boat. It seemed to hold steady in the current, and when the first stars shone forth in the darkening sky, he lay down in the boat, watching the thin sliver of the waxing moon move slowly towards the horizon.

He woke in the middle of the night. The stars shimmered and danced in the indigo sky. Rahue, his old teacher, sat in the prow of the boat. His body was luminous, and his eyes shone like silver under his white hair. He smiled at Taluhe and lifted his hand in greeting. Then he turned, pointing toward the horizon. Taluhe tried to sit up but found that he was unable to move. He wanted to call out but no sound came. He wanted to reach out to Rahue but he could not lift his hand. Rahue sat quietly, looking at him and smiling. He nodded his head briefly as if answering an unspoken question, and then his body became transparent and drifted away on the wind like morning fog.

The second day brought an absence of wind that troubled Taluhe, and he searched the horizons for signs of clouds that would give him an indication of the next day's weather. The sky was hazy and the heat heavy. He felt listless and remembered Rahue's warning to listen to the body as an important messenger of the changing of wind and weather. He could feel the early signs of a storm brewing somewhere beyond the horizon but hoped that it would not come his way. He could not sleep much during the night, searching the skies for signs of lightning and the air for signs of the coolness that would presage rain.

The early dawn brought heavy clouds crowding the line between sea and sky, and a wall of darkness rapidly rose, covering the sky. The wind blew up in gusts that quickly made him lower his fragile sail. It soon increased in force, and the waves rose to such heights that his boat seemed lost in the valleys between them. His mast broke while he rode the top of a wave. He clung to the boat's edge and the water washed over him again and again, and he could feel his body becoming cold and numb.

A giant wave picked his boat up and dropped it, throwing him free into the water. He was buried under the mass of water rolling over him, and as it pressed him down into the depth, he felt a great sadness that he had not reached his goal to see another human face before his death. His lungs burned as they filled with water and darkness closed around him. He could feel his heart beat frantically, then falter and stop.

There was a great silence. He heard no longer the churning of the water and the roaring of the storm. He felt himself floating gently and then, rising above the waves, he saw his body tumbling in the waters below. Rahue, holding his hand, smiled at him, and together they floated over the waves to a boat that sailed among silvery clouds. It seemed to be made of moonlight, with a sail shimmering like the inside of the large pink seashells Taluhe had gathered as a boy. Amantah sat in the prow of the boat, the red flowers glowing in her night-black hair, and his father and mother and the two little boys sat quietly in the back. Rahue motioned to him to take the guide's seat and, standing by the mast, he pointed towards the horizon where an island with green mountains and white beaches waited for them in the rising sun.

*   *   *

"Back already?" the angel greeted Taluhe, "Did you not leave just an instant ago?"

Taluhe looked at him in astonishment. "I lived nineteen turns of the seasons," he exclaimed.

"A fraction of an instant as time goes here," the angel smiled. "But some lessons are shorter than others. Yet much can be learned even in the briefest instant! So tell me what you think this life was about."

Taluhe sat in silence for a while. "I am not sure," he considered, "but I think it had to do with needing others. I have always wanted to be alone, away from the noise and chatter, and most of all the demands of others. When my father wanted me to become a boat builder, it would have meant constantly having to work with others, listening to them giving me orders or later being responsible for giving orders myself. I wanted to be free of that and so chose to become a boat guide. It was a way of being special and different and also gave me much time to be alone. I certainly succeeded in that," he added with a wistful smile.

"Yes, you surely did," the angel confirmed and looked thoughtful. "So what did you learn out of all this?"

Taluhe sighed. "I had all the solitude and the silence anybody could have wished for and realized how much I missed all of them. My mother and father with their demands on me, my little brothers with all their noise, the other young men whom I used to look down at because they had no interests other than fishing and making love to the young women, the old people who spent all their time recalling the big storms they survived and how brave they had been. I found that I was nothing without them, that my life did not matter unless it was part of the lives of others, that all the knowledge and skills I had learned were useless unless I put them to use for the good of others. That is why I had to try and leave the island. I had to find other people and begin to give back to them what I had to offer. But I did not succeed, did I?" he added sadly.

"You did succeed in what mattered the most," the angel replied and laid a consoling hand on Taluhe's arm. "You knew full well that you might not make it to the next island. You could have stayed on the island and lived out your life there. You had enough food and water and shelter and were quite safe there. Yet you chose to leave to find others of your kind and risked your life trying. That was your task, and you fulfilled it, rest assured. This is the first time that you chose not to stay isolated, as you have in many other lives. It is a good start, although you have more to learn in this regard." And the angel lifted his hand and pointed to a shore where a group of people was gathering to launch a large boat. "Join them" the Angel smiled. "You have another opportunity coming up right now!"

And Taluhe ran, joyfully, and with a feeling of urgency that made him feel he could fly.

"But you can if you want to," the angel's voice followed him, and so he did.

CHAPTER FIVE

The Doctor

The young doctor straightened up in the old wooden desk chair. Three more emergency room charts lay in front of her, waiting to be finished. Her eyes were burning, and the gnawing feeling in her stomach reminded her that dinner had been cut short, as usual, by a call to the emergency room. That had been at eight o'clock last night, and now it was one o'clock in the morning. She sighed and pulled the next chart closer. Her last patient, an old woman, had been brought in unable to breathe, her lips livid and her chest straining for air. It had taken an hour until she had relaxed under an injection of morphine, and the edema in her lungs had begun to subside a little. Now the patient was resting more comfortably in the cardiac unit on the second floor.

She stood up, stretched, and opened the door to the treatment room. "Any more, Lisa?" she asked the young nurse who was busy tidying up the emergency cart, checking supplies and medications.

"Nothing in the waiting room right now," the nurse replied. "Maybe we'll be lucky for a while."

She went back to the desk and began to fill out the second chart. If she hurried, she might be able to catch a catnap on the stretcher before the next patient walked into the emergency room.

Her head was drooping to her chest as she was writing, when the young nurse pushed the door open and called her: "Quick, doctor, please come quick."

She came awake with a start, bewildered for a moment, then shook herself alert and ran into the treatment room. The nurse was talking to a woman.

Late thirties, poor, recent immigrant . . . , the doctor's mind was making her usual scan. The woman was weeping, holding a baby in her arms, wrapped in a flowered quilt. The nurse was trying to take the child from her, but the woman turned to the doctor hoping to find rescue in her authority.

"Please, doctor," she said, her voice hard to hear over the weeping, "please, my baby, he was okay. Just a little while ago, he was breathing okay. But now he does not breathe. Please, doctor . . . ."

The young woman took the child gently from the mother. She laid him on the examination table. *Skin cool, no corneal reflexes, no respiration, no spontaneous movement.* She placed her stethoscope on the child's chest. *Male infant, six or seven months old,* she thought, *a little pasty, no marks of injuries, well cared for.* There was no heartbeat. "When did you find the child like this?" she asked the mother who was standing in the corner, staring wide-eyed at her. Her question set off another storm of weeping.

"I just go to my neighbor across the hall to borrow milk, just for a little. We talk, just for a little. The baby was sleeping, really good; he had drunk all his milk. I was with the neighbor, just a little. I come back and I think he is sleeping so good, and then I see he does not look right. He does not breathe. Please, doctor, make him breathe again."

Cribdeath, the young doctor thought, and her heart was heavy. *It's always the same story. Nothing seems wrong, and then suddenly there is nothing—no cry, no struggle, just nothing. How do I tell her that he will never breathe again, her lovely little boy?* She turned wearily to the nurse. "Call a code. We will try, at least," and she bent over the child to start the resuscitation process.

An hour later, she left the treatment room. The code team had done everything possible, knowing full well that there was no real hope. The child had been found too late, the trip to the hospital had taken too long, but they had tried anyway. She walked over to the woman who had been standing in the waiting room, her hands clenched together, not letting the door to the treatment room out of her sight for a moment. She put her arm around the mother's shoulder. "Come," she said gently, "Come, sit down here. Your son, he will not breathe again. There is nothing we can do anymore to make him breathe again."

The woman stared at her in disbelief. "No, no, he was all right, just a little while ago. No, please, please help him. You are a doctor. You can help him."

She led the weeping woman into the treatment room to a chair, pushing her down gently. Then turning to the nurse who stood in the doorway eyes brimming with tears, she said, "Get us some coffee, Lisa, or tea, anything hot, lots of sugar. And see if anybody came with her."

The woman sat slumped in the chair, stunned by the blow. Then she rose and walked over to the examination table. She lifted the child into her arms and stared at him. "Baby," she murmured, "my little one . . . ."

*   *   *

United States, 19th Century

Jonathan awoke with a start. He had fallen asleep at the kitchen table. The petroleum lamp was burning low, throwing shadows on the white walls. He stood up, stiff and aching, and stepped up to the bedroom door. His mother had fallen asleep in the rocking chair, holding his baby sister tight in her arms. The child had fallen ill with the same brain fever that had taken his father three weeks ago, and his mother, exhausted from caring for the big man who had fought and screamed in delirium for days, had refused the offer of the doctor to get a nurse.

"She is my child and I will care for her. She would be scared of strangers. I won't have it."

Doc McFarland had shaken his head and had muttered about stubborn German women. But he drove over to their farm every day, and spent time with Emma Werner and Jonathan and little Elsie, who was only two and who did not recognize anyone now.

Jonathan bent over the child. "She is not breathing," he suddenly realized with a shiver. "Oh my God, she is not breathing. Mom," he whispered urgently, "please, Mom, wake up. Elsie, she is not right."

His mother's eyes opened slowly. She stared at him without recognition.

"Mom," his voice was urgent now, "please, Mom, look at Elsie, she does not look right."

Her mother turned her glance at the child in her lap. She suddenly sat up straight, holding the child to the light. She held her upright and shook her a little. "Elsie," she called out, "Elsie, my little girl, please wake up!"

Jonathan laid his hand on her shoulder. "Mom, I think she is dead. I think Elsie has gone with Pa now, Mom."

His mother turned to him angrily. "How can you say that!? What do you know!? She is asleep, surely. She was so tired from all the crying. She is sleeping surely."

She pressed the child close to her, rocking her with her whole body. "Wake up, my little one, please wake up for your Mummy." But finally the limpness of the little child brought the message to her body that her mind wanted to refuse. She sat back in the chair, staring at her daughter. Her eyes went to Jonathan, who stood with his hands helplessly hanging at his side.

"What will we do now, Johnny?" she whispered, "Oh dear Lord, what will we do now?"

Her helplessness brought Jonathan back to action. "Give me the baby, Mom," he said gently. "Come, give her to me. I will put her in her bed, and get Mrs. Taylor to stay with you, and then I get the buggy and go get Doc." He led the dry-eyed woman to the bed and covered her with a heavy quilt. He laid the child in the small bed by the window, like he had when she had fallen asleep on his shoulder in the evening.

His mother lay like one dead, her eyes open, staring at the ceiling.

Jonathan bent over her. "I will be right back," he said. "Just waking Mrs. Taylor."

They had the funeral the next day because the August heat made a delay impossible. His mother had remained silent, moving about like a sleepwalker. Doc McFarland had examined her and then took Jonathan aside.

"Exhaustion, grief, shock—you name it, she had it," he grumbled, running his hand through his reddish hair that would never lie down properly. "Nothing that time and some good care won't cure. But where will she get that? It's harvest coming up, and with your father dead, how will you two run the farm? You are only sixteen, and help is hard to get these days on such short notice."

Jonathan shook his head. "I don't know, Doc, I haven't had time to think straight since Dad got sick."

The doctor looked at him sharply. "When have you had your last decent meal?" he questioned.

"I can't remember. I would cook for us, but then something

always happened, so I never got to eat much of it. Neither did Mom, come to think."

The doctor shook his head. "You both," he said, "pack up some clothes. You come with me for the week and let my housekeeper make you some decent food. Nothing fancy, but good, and plenty of it." And ignoring Jonathan's protest and his mother's lethargy, he had them packing and in his carriage within the hour.

By Christmas time, they had auctioned off the farm. The harvest had been good, but the bank had not been willing to extend their loan payments in view of Jonathan's father's death. His mother had taken two months to regain some semblance of being alive again.

They moved into town, renting two rooms in the house of another widow, and his mother began to take in sewing jobs. She had some skill at doing fancy sewing and soon the ladies in town would come to her with pictures of dresses that ladies wore in the big town, and Mrs. Werner would spent her days and often half of the night cutting and stitching satins and silks.

Jonathan took on delivering groceries or chopping firewood and any other jobs he could find, and somehow life began to take on some rhythm of normality again. He loved to spend the evenings reading to his mother while she sewed. Doc McFarland had given Jonathan the use of his extensive library, which contained not only huge volumes of anatomy and medicine, but also books of philosophy and literature and a beautiful collection of poetry.

It was in the second year after Jonathan's father's death that Doc McFarland took a long-deserved vacation and went to Boston to attend a medical meeting. He was gone for a month, leaving his practice to be covered by the only other doctor in town, a younger man with what McFarland called "new-fangled ideas" about medicine.

When he returned, he set the town astir with the news that he had brought back with him a new wife. Having been a widower for more than ten years and showing himself resistant to any attempts of the local eligible females to be married off again, this raised considerable consternation and curiosity. It quickly became known that the new Mrs. McFarland was much younger than Doc, who was in his mid-forties. She was also said to be very beautiful, charming, and educated.

Jonathan and his mother heard little of the local gossip, having limited contact with the people whose favorite activity was to spread such news around town.

In the middle of May, Jonathan took a delivery of sewing to the wife of the Reverend Perlin, this time cotton blouses rather than silk dresses, as Mrs. Perlin held little value in overly fancy clothes, and her husband's income did not allow any female extravagances.

Jonathan gathered several books of poetry that he had borrowed from McFarland quite a while ago. After having made his delivery to the minister's wife, he took himself over to the doctor's house. The three-storied white house was well set back from the street, with a group of flowering lilac bushes nearly hiding the steep steps leading up to the private entrance at the side of the house. The doctor kept his office on the ground floor, and Jonathan, as usual, ran up the stairs and knocked perfunctorily, knowing that Mrs. Dellman, Doc's elderly housekeeper, was a little hard of hearing, and went, as usual, straight through the hallway into the library.

At his somewhat stormy entry, a young woman in a long white cotton dress dotted with small green flowers rose from a heavy leather chair, measuring him with cool gray eyes. Her dark auburn hair fell freely over her shoulders, halfway to her waist. "Hello," she said, "and who may I say is calling?"

Jonathan stood rooted to the ground. He had heard of Doc's

marriage, but somehow it never had become real to him. Until now, that is.

Joanna McFarland, seeing his confusion, relented. "Come, sit down," she said, and taking the books from his hand, she looked at them. "I see you and Frederic have something in common— your love for poetry at least."

Frederic? Jonathan realized that in all the years he had known Doc McFarland, he had never heard anyone call him by his Christian name.

Jonathan sank into the other leather chair. "I am sorry," he muttered. "I am a fool, I did not think . . . . I am Jonathan Werner, Doc took care of my father . . . ." He was at a loss to explain himself without saying something that might sound completely foolish to this cool, gray-eyed young woman in white.

"Oh, I know," she said lightly, "I have been quite a surprise to most people in town. They did not know that Frederic and my late husband and I were friends for years, and after he died, we stayed in touch by letter. So when he came back to Boston, it seemed the right thing to do, to get married. But it must have looked quite unseemly and hasty to the good folks in town here."

Her words put Jonathan at ease, and his confusion subsided. He laughed and rose and, bowing with some formality, said, "Thank you for your kind reception. I hope I did not surprise you too much, storming in here like this. Doc gave me permission to borrow any books I wanted from the library. But I promise, I will knock the next time."

She rose too, walking back with him through the cool hallway to the entrance. "I enjoyed meeting you," she said. "Next time, maybe you can tell me what poets you love the most. There are not that many people in this town who know much about poetry, and Frederic is so busy."

There was a shadow of sadness in her voice, and Jonathan looked at her sharply. But she was opening the door for him, said a friendly good-bye, and was gone behind the lace curtains of the front door.

Jonathan found little time for reading or visiting Doc's library during the next weeks. He had taken on a job helping with the construction of a barn, and after one man was injured by a falling beam, there was little time to spare if they were to finish the job before harvest time. But he found himself thinking often of cool gray eyes and auburn hair falling over a white dress.

He was on his way home one evening when Doc McFarland reined in his horse carriage beside him. "Jonathan, how are things going?" he called out. "Haven't seen you, I don't remember when the last. Heard you nearly ran Joanna down a while back."

Jonathan grinned, wiping his face with his jacket sleeve. It was a heavy, hot evening, and thunderclouds had been gathering at the horizon all afternoon.

"Come, hop up, boy," the doctor said. "I'll give you a ride home."

Jonathan gratefully climbed up on the seat beside the doctor and the two passed the ride home with Doc asking about Jonathan's and his mother's welfare. They passed the doctor's house on the way to Jonathan's home, and McFarland handed the reins to Jonathan. "Wait for me," he said. "Need to check for messages." He was back five minutes later, cursing under his breath.

"I should have known better than to stop. Should have gone to the saloon and had a beer with you instead. Now I have to drive all the way out toward Stanton Station where this poor soul of a wife to that damned drunkard Ferris is having another baby." His angry voice was hoarse with weariness, and Jonathan felt pity with the older man.

"Let me come with you, Doc," he said, "I can drive part of the way, and you can sleep a little."

McFarland turned to him. "Thank you, Jonathan," he said gratefully. "That would be a big help."

By sunset, they had arrived at the small cluster of houses five miles outside of town. The thunderclouds had grown, and lightning flashed on the horizon. The two men entered the small ramshackle house that had a poor little vegetable garden attached to its side, and a small flock of discouraged-looking chickens still scratched in the dry dust.

Inside the house was dark except for the light of a small candle. It showed them a group of four children staring at them in silence, the oldest no more than seven, the youngest barely two, with dirty faces and lanky hair, huddled around an unlit stove.

A man lay snoring in an old cane chair, his breath heavy with the smell of cheap liquor. He had been good-looking once, but there was a cruel line to his mouth even in the laxness of his drunkenness.

A door was ajar, leading to a small bedroom where another candle gave just enough light to help them find their way to the woman on the bed, her hands gripping the sides of the bedstead, her breath coming hard and straining. Her eyes lit up at the sight of Doc McFarland.

"Oh God, I am so glad you could come, Doc. It is not going right this time. It never took this long."

McFarland stepped up to the bed, taking her hands and feeling her pulse. "When did the pains start, Mary?" he inquired.

"My water broke this morning and the pains started soon after. But they are just getting worse and worse, and the baby should have come by now." She sank back exhausted into the pillows.

"Jonathan, see if you can rouse that drunken bastard or find some way to light that stove and heat some water to boil. I need to examine her. The baby may be in the wrong position."

It took an hour for Doc McFarland to deliver the exhausted woman of a breech birth. The baby had trouble breathing, but in the end found its way into the world with a weak, whining cry.

McFarland looked at Jonathan. "Should castrate that bastard out there," he muttered. "A year from now she will have another one, and each time, she will be weaker and more undernourished, and the kids will be just the same. There is no end to the misery that people will create for themselves and their children."

He packed up his instruments and, holding the woman's thin hands in his, he smiled at her with a gentleness that surprised Jonathan. "Mary," he said, "can't you go back to your family? Take the kids and get away from here."

The woman looked at him and shook her head. "They would not take me back, Doc," she whispered. "They warned me and I would not listen. And there is no place else to go."

The two men stepped into the night, savoring the clean smell of the wind that was bringing the storm. McFarland's voice shook with outrage. "She was beautiful once. Came from an educated family. Fell in love with this good-for-nothing who put on a show with fancy clothes and fancy talk and who probably thought she'd come with some money. When she refused the reasonable marriage her parents had arranged for her with an older man, they cut her off without a penny. She wanted love and romance. Look at her now!"

"But people can't help falling in love," Jonathan protested.

McFarland's face was grim. "No, I guess we poor fools can't help that. But we could at least use the brains the good Lord gave us to consider what will be left when the flash fire is burnt down and the romance is getting tattered at the edges. Most people would do much better for themselves in marriage by using more common sense and a good dose of mutual respect than falling for melting smiles and charming looks."

The thunderstorm broke when they were three miles away from town. They had to stop the carriage, and Jonathan had to lead the frightened horse with its eyes covered while the flashes struck the ground in the fields all around them. They were both soaked to the skin when they arrived at the doctor's house. The older man was so exhausted that Jonathan nearly carried him up the steps. Joanna opened the door for them.

"She must have been waiting for him," Jonathan thought. "It must be after midnight, and she stayed up waiting."

He helped her undress McFarland, who was shaking and muttering to himself and who, after a hot rum toddy, fell instantly and deeply asleep. Jonathan sat in the kitchen drinking tea with rum, when Joanna came down the stairs carrying McFarland's wet and dirty clothes.

"Get out of your wet things," she said. "You will catch your death." She handed him an old dressing gown and a blanket. "Dry off and then get to sleep in the guest room. It is right off the library. There is no sense in going out again into this storm."

Jonathan looked at her. She looked tired and drawn, but there was another expression in her face he could not read. "He'll be all right again tomorrow," he said. "He's just worn out. He cares so much for people, and he feels so helpless sometimes."

Joanna stared at him, and suddenly her eyes filled with tears. "Yes," she said, and her voice shook, "he cares so much, and he is killing himself." And suddenly she was weeping uncontrollably, her hands pressed to her face to stifle her sobs.

Jonathan reached out to touch her shaking shoulder. "Please," he pleaded, "really, he'll be all right again tomorrow."

Joanna turned to him suddenly, her eyes angry. "If he dies," she said, and her voice was bitter, "do you realize that he will be the second man I have loved who killed himself because he cared so much for others? And didn't remember he had a wife," she added as an afterthought.

Jonathan looked at her. "My God, how beautiful she is," he thought suddenly and continued to stare at her as if he was seeing her for the first time.

She felt his stare and looked up at him. "Thank you for bringing him home," she said softly, "and I am sorry for making a scene. I got so scared waiting all night for him in that thunderstorm, and I am tired."

Jonathan stood, unable to move. Joanna stepped up to him. "Jonathan?" she said. "Jonathan . . . ," and suddenly she was in his arms, crying again and holding on to him as if asking for help. He covered her face with kisses, awkwardly at first, but soon caught up in a fire that seemed to consume his whole body. They were both trembling, and in the end, they made love on the narrow bed in the guest room behind the library.

Jonathan awoke in the morning, sunlight streaming through the muslin curtains of the guest room windows. He could not remember where he was at first, but then the events of the night rushed back into his mind and he groaned.

He still sat on the bed, holding his head, when Joanna walked in briskly, carrying a tray with steaming coffee and freshly baked buns. She set the tray on the table by his bed and sat down beside him. Jonathan raised his eyes to her. She looked as beautiful and cool in her white dress as always, and she smiled at him.

"How is Doc?" Jonathan tried to ask, but he had to clear his voice twice to get the words out.

"Out making his rounds, fit as a fiddle," she smiled. "He asked about you, and I told him you were sleeping off last night's extravaganza. He asked me to thank you for bringing him home last night. He felt he would not have made it back by himself."

"You told him?" Jonathan's voice could not hide his disbelief. "About last night?"

Joanna looked at him for a long time. "No, Jonathan" she said. "I did not, and I won't. Being a doctor, he probably would understand what could happen between two exhausted and frightened people. But he is also a man, and not a young one anymore, and it would hurt him a lot."

Jonathan shook his head. "I love this man like my own father," he said slowly, "but I think I love you, too. I have not been able to get you out of my mind since I first saw you in that library. What are we going to do, Joanna?"

"Right now, you will have some breakfast and get dressed," she said firmly. "I sent a message to your mother so she won't be worried to death about you. What happened last night—happened."

Jonathan stayed away from Doctor McFarland's house for two weeks. Then the doctor sent for him one evening, asking if he would help him drive out to one of the outlying farms where a farm helper had been badly hurt when a cart turned over, pinning his leg beneath a wheel. Jonathan spent much of that night holding Doc's instruments and wiping blood, while they amputated the man's leg. Afterward, McFarland looked at Jonathan for a long time. "You would make a good doctor, boy," he said. "Steady hands and a strong stomach and no fuss. Have you ever thought about it?"

Jonathan looked at him. "I have sometimes wished I could," he said, "first when Dad and Elsie died, and then when I saw that poor woman Mary Ferris with one baby after another. There is so much to learn and so many things we don't know yet. But there is no way now, with just Mom and me, and her having nobody else to look after her. There is no money for that kind of schooling."

"Let's talk about money later," McFarland said gruffly. "I am not a rich man, but I am not a beggar either. If you really want this, we can find a way."

After that, Jonathan began to accompany Doc on many of his evening and night calls and McFarland took pleasure in his quick mind and good memory. He was particularly impressed with Jonathan's ability to remain steady and able to function in a critical situation. They talked much about Jonathan's future and what kind of education Jonathan would need to be acceptable to a medical school. McFarland suggested that Jonathan apply to a medical school in Boston, where McFarland knew people who might be able to assist the boy with his plans.

Whenever Jonathan saw Joanna in the doctor's house, she was warm and friendly, but showed with neither sign nor word that she wanted to remember the night of the thunderstorm.

It was a cold, foggy night in late October when McFarland and Jonathan came back very late from a difficult delivery seven miles out of town. The horse had mis-stepped and become lame, and it had begun to rain heavily on their way home. McFarland suggested that Jonathan sleep over at their house that night.

It was long after midnight. Jonathan was still reading by the light of a small lamp by his bedside, listening to the storm beating leaves and small branches against the windows, and thinking of Joanna, when the door to his room opened.

She stood in the doorway, holding a candle. The flickering flame threw moving shadows over her face, and she looked as if she had cried. Jonathan sat up staring at her. She moved swiftly over to his bed, blew out the candle and extinguished the little lamp.

"I need to be with you," she whispered. "I have been alone so long. I just had to come."

"But Doc . . . ," Jonathan's voice was hoarse.

"Frederic is asleep, as always. He falls into bed when he comes home like this, which is most evenings, and does not move again until sunup." Her voice was pleading. "Do you know what it is like to lie night after night looking at a man too tired and too worn out by other people's troubles to remember that he has a wife?" She was crying now, and Jonathan held her close.

"I love Frederic, but I should not have married him. His work leaves no space for another person."

Jonathan could feel the warmth of her body and the softness of her breasts against him. He thought of McFarland, sleeping the sleep of exhaustion in his bed, and of the kindness the older man had shown him for years, and then his body responded to the murmur of her voice, and her pleading hands caressing him, and nothing else mattered much.

After this, Joanna came to his room whenever he stayed at McFarland's house, and with winter coming on and the two men often coming home late and chilled to their bones, this became more frequent. During the days, Jonathan felt tormented by guilt and doubts, and each time McFarland complimented him or spoke with growing enthusiasm about medical school, he felt that he wanted to run as far as his legs would carry him to get away from his betrayal. But at night when he held Joanna in his arms, he thought of her loveliness, and nothing seemed to matter but their passion.

It was in April, after they had made love again in a stormy spring night, with the wind blowing the smell of wet earth and growing things into the open window, that Joanna told him she was carrying his child. Jonathan stared at her in the light of the small lamp.

"Are you sure it is my child?" he said slowly.

"Quite sure," she said. "Frederic has not come near me in more than two months."

"What will you tell him?" Jonathan's voice was hoarse, and he could feel his insides twisting into a painful knot.

"I will try to have him make love to me this week," she said calmly. "I have wanted a child ever since I realized that his life is so completely filled with caring for others. He does not have to know that it is not his. He will love it anyway."

Jonathan stared at her. He trembled and was filled with a dark sorrow that made him want to cry. He stood up and got dressed.

"Where are you going?" she said. "It's still raining out there."

"I need to walk and think," he murmured, and quietly let himself out of the house.

He did not see Joanna for the next week, and he found it hard to think clearly. His love for Joanna and his deep feelings for Doc, his sense of guilt and betrayal, his longing for her body, the thought of her bearing his child—all this became a turmoil of confusion in his mind, and he could not see a way to continue his life with these two people who had become so important to him.

In the first week of May, he accompanied McFarland to a farm where three of the children had come down with mumps. The children seemed on the road to recovery, and on the way back to town, McFarland reviewed with Jonathan the symptoms and the course of the illness.

"It is good for them to have the mumps as children," he said slowly. "If they get it as adults, I have found that it can render men sterile and unable to father children. It happened to me that way, and it was a great sorrow to my first wife. I have seen it several times in couples where the woman was blamed for being barren, but when she was widowed young, she had healthy children with another husband."

Jonathan felt his whole body shake. So McFarland was sterile and he knew it. *He never told Joanna*, he thought angrily. *He should have told her before he married her.*

"When we talked about marriage, Joanna did not feel that children were all that important to her," McFarland continued, as if answering Jonathan's thoughts, "so I decided not to tell her. It is not an easy thing to admit for a man."

Jonathan suddenly looked with pity at the older man. He had never thought of McFarland as other than Doc, who drove out day and night to deliver babies or set broken bones or dress burns and wounds or sit with a fevered child all night. He had never thought of him as a man who could feel hurt and shame like any other, and his heart ached with sudden compassion.

Then the immensity of what McFarland had just said impressed itself on Jonathan, and he knew that he could never bear to face him again once McFarland knew about Joanna's pregnancy.

He knew that he would have to leave them both and give up their friendship and his dream of becoming a doctor, and he hoped that somehow they would find a bridge across the pain and the hurt that would come between them. He had no place there anymore.

He drove McFarland back to his house, wished him good night, and suddenly, overwhelmed with sorrow and regret, took the older man by his shoulders. "Doc," and his voice trembled, "Doc, since my father died, you have been the best friend I have ever had." He turned abruptly and swiftly walked into the gathering dusk.

McFarland looked after him for a long time. "Jonathan," he said softly to himself, "you could have been the son I would have wanted for myself. I hope I can raise your child with love."

When Jonathan arrived at home, his mother was asleep at the table, her sewing slipped from her hands. Jonathan woke her and helped her to bed. He kissed her good night and stroked her silvering hair. Jonathan spent hours trying to write her a letter that could make her understand what he was about to do without telling her what had happened.

In the end, he left a brief note telling her that Doc had called on him late and asked him to drive to Boston to pick up some new medicines.

He packed a few clothes and the money he had saved that winter from his jobs. At dawn, he left the house and walked quickly down the main road. When he passed McFarland's house, he saw a light in the kitchen and he knew that Doc was up and getting ready for his morning rounds.

He thought of the future and the hopes that were no longer his, and of the opportunity lost and the friend betrayed, and he wondered what he would do with his life now. He thought of Joanna carrying his child and being reminded of him every time she looked at it, and he wondered if she would be able to love it.

He thought of McFarland, who cared so much for people and who had been afraid to tell his beautiful young wife that he could father no children and so had stayed away from her until she had sought consolation with a young man who had fallen in love with her bright young beauty and her cool gray eyes. He thought of his mother who had been so proud of his new dream and of the long, lonely years ahead of her.

He thought of Mary Ferris and her sad children, and he suddenly knew that, even if he could not become a doctor, he could still use his mind and his energy and his love for people to help ease their misery and relieve some of their suffering. There would be many other ways he could do that.

It began to rain gently, a warm spring rain that fell on the young green grain in the fields, and Jonathan was glad, for the raindrops mixed with the tears that he could not stop, and it cooled his face.

*   *   *

Jonathan looked around in amazement. "I did not expect there to be anything after death," he exclaimed.

"And why not," the angel asked with raised eyebrows, or what served for eyebrows in an angel.

"Well, there has been no scientific proof of the existence of the soul or God or anything," Jonathan said.

"Really?" said the angel lightly, "Did it ever occur to you that it may not be possible to 'prove' divine energy with the crude instruments your so-called scientists have been using? But if you just used your common sense, should not the very existence of life, of procreation, of the body's ability to heal, of the beauty in nature be enough evidence of divine energy and order? And in any case, here you are now, so that is all the proof you need, isn't it?"

Jonathan nodded, still looking somewhat bewildered.

"Tell, me," said the angel, "last time I checked in on you, you were running away again from your responsibilities, leaving behind a woman pregnant with your child. What did you do after that?"

"What do you mean, checked in on me? Why would you do that?"

"That is my affair," the angel said a bit curtly.

Jonathan looked at the angel and the angel looked back at him in silence. The silence lasted for what seemed like a small eternity, until finally Jonathan sighed.

"I went to the next small town and hired out for a while as a farm worker. It was something I knew how to do. I realized very soon that this was not what I wanted to do with my life, so I made friends with a teacher at the school there and he began to help me become a teacher in mathematics and sciences."

"Ah," said the angel, "therefore the scientific approach to life!"

Jonathan frowned. "I was a good teacher," he said, "and I cared about my students, and they liked me. Maybe as I got older, I became a little stricter than necessary, but the children seemed to become more and more undisciplined, and it was harder to get them interested in learning. I married a young woman when I was forty and we had two children. I am not sure they liked me very much, and I often wondered if my wife really loved me or just married me to get married."

"Did you love her?" the angel asked.

"I cared for her; she was a good wife, and she did love our children. Maybe I never showed her enough that I cared. I don't know."

"Was it the life you wanted for yourself?" the angel asked softly.

Jonathan was quiet for a long time. "No," he finally answered sadly, "not at all. Somehow, when I left Joanna and Doc, I left behind so much else. I loved them both so very much, and somehow I never let myself really love anybody else after that. But what could I have possibly done under the circumstances?"

"What could you have done?" the angel repeated and fell silent.

This time the silence lasted even longer.

"Maybe I could have stayed and continued to help Doc, and if he did not want me around, then I could have left. Maybe I could have gone back later to see how they were doing, and to see the child. I never dared, somehow. My mother joined me before the child was born, so I never found out what happened. Maybe I did not really want to know."

"Do you want to know now?" the angel asked.

Jonathan stared in front of him. "Yes, I think I do," he said quietly. "I think I need to know."

"Yes, you do," the angel agreed. "Joanna had a boy, a beautiful child. Doc knew she was pregnant even before she told him, and knew it was yours, even before you left. He had heard you two making love one night when you thought he was asleep. He did not mind as much as you were afraid he would. He knew how lonely Joanna had been because of his work. And he knew he could not give her a child, and felt a child from you he could accept. He was sad that you left, and Joanna was bitter that you never even made contact with her later. Doc died of a heart attack when the child was seven, and Joanna had a hard time raising him alone. There was not much money, given Doc's habit of treating many people for free. So she remarried, not difficult for a woman still young and beautiful. Her husband was wealthy; she made sure of it this time. After all, she was 'doing this for the child.' But he was a very controlling man and gave her no freedom to be herself and express her free spirit. So she left him and struggled on her own, becoming more bitter and lonely, unwilling, like you, to love people again."

"And the boy?" Jonathan hesitated, "What became of the boy?"

"He was killed in a war. He was only nineteen. He died in a ditch by the side of the road, alone."

"Poor Joanna," Jonathan sighed deeply, and he felt grief welling up in him like a dark wave that threatened to engulf him.

"You accumulated quite a burden this life," the Angel said quietly. "You threw away an opportunity to become a healer like Doc and learn from him and help him. He might have lived longer with a helper at his side. You abandoned Joanna and the child, and both lives were deeply affected by this. You owe them both."

"But they are all dead," Jonathan cried out. "How can I make amends now?"

"Nobody is dead forever," the angel smiled for the first time. "You will have plenty of opportunity to make amends, although the conditions may be a bit harder the next time. You were a teacher, right? Have you not had a student repeat a grade once or even twice? And did you not push him even harder the next time to make sure he would make it this time? Well, it is about the same here."

Jonathan looked at the angel in amazement. "You mean, there is more than one life we live?"

"Jonathan," the angel said softly, "Jonathan, wake up and remember!"

And like a flood, all his past lifetimes emerged in his soul, and he gazed in wonder and awe at the richness and variety of his own experiences and the many links in so many lives between him and the people he loved.

"Angel," he said after a long while, "why don't we remember our other lives? Would it not be helpful to know about them in making decisions?"

The angel looked at him thoughtfully. "Sometimes you do remember, when it is needful," he said. "Sometimes, in a special situation you may remember that you have repeated a pattern over and over again, and this may help you to make a different choice. But most of the time, it would be very confusing and only make it harder for you to deal with the present life. Imagine if you were to remember that your son had been your father in another life, and that he was very brutal to you. Would it not be difficult for you to raise him with love and care and not take out on him the pain and suffering you might remember?"

"Yes, I can understand that," Jonathan said quietly. "It would be nearly impossible. Is this why sometimes we feel a strong dislike for a person, or a strong attraction, even though we don't really know them well?"

"Yes," said the angel, "you do recognize each other, even though your minds do not always understand it. And the energy of your past actions will attract you to those people to whom you owe a debt or are bound to by love or hate. This will give you an opportunity to bring the energies back into balance and begin to transform hate into love. That is the most important task on your path of return to God, for how can you hope to dwell in him who is Love unless you are Love? So you realize that you have much work to do in your next lives to heal the hurts that you have inflicted and take on the responsibilities you shied away from in this last one."

"Yes," Jonathan said, and a burden lifted from his heart, "yes, I will make amends."

"Good," said the angel briskly, "then you better get to it. And Jonathan, next time, try to develop a sense of humor. You have a tendency to take yourself much too serious! It becomes irritating after a while."

CHAPTER SIX

The Prince

The young woman leaned back into the sparse shadow of the stone wall behind her. The afternoon sun in the high mountain air burned her bare shoulders. The others had found shady spots under the few scraggly trees on the main court of the pyramid. She could not see them from her perch, and it felt as if she had the whole world to herself. She gazed at the ball court below her. The short grass covering the ground was now burnt yellow in the dry season. Further away, some white cows were resting within the walls of old living quarters, seeking relief from the heat. The only moving creatures were a group of goats climbing over the partly uncovered steps of the tall pyramid on her right, grazing on small prickly bushes and thistles. A bird of prey was circling high up in the air in ever-widening spirals. It was very quiet, and even the song of the crickets was subdued.

Ethan had gone to explore the hillsides on the other side of the ruins. The altitude of the high plateau had brought back the pain in his chest, and she worried about his unrelenting energy that drove him to climb in this heat.

She had felt inexplicably sad and troubled ever since they had come on this trip to Mexico. She loved the country and the people. But since the day when they had driven before sunset to the tall hill they called the Poet King's mountain, she had felt this sadness. The mountain had a beautiful circular walk just below the mountaintop, passing by baths and stone steps carved into the sheer rock, and half-restored temples and stone figures that reminded her of Egypt.

Little white flowers she had never seen anywhere else grew out of the dusty hard earth, and beautiful, large white blossoms shimmered in the dusk on the dry hillsides. Ethan had said that this mountain had been the summer residence of an Aztec king, and that it had been famous for its gardens. She had wondered if these flowers were the offspring of those long lost gardens. That was when the sadness had risen in her like a dark wave, and she had wanted to cry.

Today, they had come to this place, which had been a vast Temple City before the Spanish conquered the country. She sat quietly, letting her gaze wander over the plateau. *Xochicalco, the White City,* she thought. It must have been beautiful when it was alive. They had seen the stone carvings on the large pyramid in the main courtyard, the plumed snakes of Quetzalcuatl. They had sat quietly in the underground observatory to watch the sun at noon shine straight down into the opening, suddenly lighting up the whole underground chamber with gold.

"That is why I wanted us to come today, on the summer solstice," Ethan had smiled. The old guard had enjoyed their marveling at the skill of the old culture and had shared his stories about the discovery and the reconstruction of the pyramids that he had been part of in his youth.

She saw Ethan climbing down the steps of the large pyramid

and continuing on to the ball court. He stood for a moment on the upper steps and then jumped down the stone stairs two and three at a time, and she had to laugh at his irrepressible exuberance. She thought of the recent years and all the hard work they had done together developing a center to help young people learn and grow. She had felt so exhausted and overwhelmed at times that she sometimes longed to find a quiet place by herself and withdraw from all the demands life was making on her. She looked at their friends resting in the shade in the upper courtyard, thinking of the years they all had spent together, growing closer in their shared work and friendship. She thought of her little son, already three, left at home with his grandmother. These trips were good for the nourishing of the spirit, she thought, but they would have been a little rough on three-year-old legs.

Ethan was standing in the ball court, raising his hand in greeting, as he saw her sitting on the ledge of the small temple.

"My prince," a small voice seemed to whisper in her, "my prince . . . ."

*   *   *

Mexico, circa 1400 AD

The old priest sat on the ledge of the small temple watching the ballgame come to a close. Neza's team had won this time, and the players were carrying him on their shoulders to the exit of the court. He saw Xihu sitting above him and raised his hand in greeting. The feathers of his headdress shone blue-green in the fierce sunlight. Like a crown of moonlight, Xihu thought. He smiled. The players would go and bathe and then feast until sunset. He hoped that Neza would remember that they had planned to go down into the village later that night to buy some healing herbs from the old wise woman. But Neza always remembered.

He turned to climb down the steps to the living quarters. His knees hurt more today. "Years and years of going up and down steep stairs will wear out anybody's bones before their time," Xihu thought. "I have been climbing these stairs since I was seven." He remembered clearly the day his father took him from their small hut in the village far below the big white Temple City that had always seemed to him the City of the Gods. His mother had cried but had looked proud at the same time, and his older sister had embraced him and told him to be good and to remember her. He had done so for many years. She died in childbirth the same year he entered into full priesthood. He could still see her the way she looked as a girl, tall and beautiful, with very long, shiny black hair that she always loved to adorn with wild flowers.

He entered into his cool dark room. It was a relief after the brightness of the sun outside. He filled a small bowl with cool water from the water pot and sank gratefully down on the pallet. He wondered how the feasting was proceeding. The last time Neza's team had won, they all had drunk so much pulque that they were ill for two days. He hoped Neza remembered that, too.

He thought of the day Neza had been brought to the Sacred City. He had been a small boy, no more than seven or eight summers old. Several warriors had come with him, some of them badly wounded. Nobody spoke about Neza's family, but Xihu had recognized the colors of the warriors' plumed coats. Later, they had heard rumors that the king of Texcoco had been killed in a raid by another tribe, and that his son had escaped with several trustworthy members of the king's bodyguard.

Neza had never spoken about his early years, and Xihu had never ventured to ask. The priest had taken pity on the child who had appeared grieving and lonely, and had befriended him. Neza had grown into a tall, handsome youth and had absorbed as much of the knowledge the Sacred City had to offer as the high priest had thought fit for him to learn. Xihu had also given him the knowledge that was only taught to priests. He had always felt that Neza was meant to be a priest and was therefore entitled to this knowledge. Neza had taken this knowledge also and kept it in his heart, together with the secrets of his past.

When he was twelve, he had accompanied Xihu to one of the southern temple cities, and there had befriended one of the priests learned in the ways of the stars and their cycles. Neza had stayed there for two years to study. He had come back not only grown in stature but also in inner strength, and was more solitary than before. From that time on he would spend many hours, during the days as well as at night, walking and climbing the surrounding hillsides, only returning to his quarters in the temple after sunrise.

A few times, he had taken of the sacred mushrooms and spent a week alone in the mountains to the north. He had come back from those journeys with a look of transparency that Xihu could not explain only as lack of food and sleep. Neza had shared with him only that he had visions that had shaken him to the core of his being, but would not speak more of them.

In the past months he had received a growing number of visitors whom Xihu thought to be persons of high station. There had been many meetings, often until late at night, and finally Neza had confided in Xihu that members of his father's family wanted their young prince to return.

Xihu sighed. The thought of losing his young friend was much more painful to consider than he would have expected. "It is like losing the son I never had," he thought sadly.

When Neza entered his room, Xihu rose from a light sleep.

"Come, old friend." The young man knelt down to offer him a hand in rising. "It is time to go down to the village. The sun has set and the wind comes cool from the valley. Let us find the old woman and ask her if she has herbs to soothe your aching bones. Our healer here has not been very helpful to you these past months."

Xihu smiled. His friend was not known to be very tolerant with incompetent people, be they healers, ballplayers or cooks. He demanded from them what he demanded from himself—intense effort and perfection. "If he is to become king he needs to learn patience," he thought to himself. "Not everybody has his strength and beauty and quick mind."

They called a boy to carry a torch for them and began the

descent to the village. Xihu had to reach for Neza's arm for support during their descent, and found his legs shaking at the bottom of the steep hill.

"We should have taken a litter," Neza said apologetically.

"I am not that old and frail yet," Xihu protested, and set off at a brisk pace on the path to the small houses nestling under some dark trees. Only a few were still lit by small oil lamps. The old wise woman lived in a house at the end of the village, a little set apart from the others. She was sitting in front of her door, quietly watching the rising moon. When she saw the two men approaching, she nodded her head briefly and motioned for them to sit down beside her.

"It is a good night for mixing healing herbs," she said in a soft voice that sounded amazingly young in a body so wrinkled that it reminded Xihu of a dried fruit. "The moon is full and it is gentle. But you, old priest, take this blanket and cover your knees with it. The night air draws the life out of your bones and the chill will dampen the fire of your blood."

She rose and went into her hut to return a little while later with a bowl that steamed and spread a pungent aroma. "It is bitter, but less bitter than your pains. Drink this now. I will give you herbs to take with you. Steep them in boiling water and drink of them each night until the next full moon, and cover your bones at night with a blanket. And use a stick or the arm of a servant when you climb those sacred stairs up there. You need to take your body's weight off your bones for a while."

Xihu could see Neza's smile in the bright moonlight as he bent towards the old woman. "Honored mother," he said, "if I am ever in need of a healer, may I call for you? Your wisdom far surpasses that of many healers in temple or kingly court, because you use the wisdom of everyday life."

The old woman looked at him long and steadily. "Prince," her voice trembled a little, "Prince, you will not need me for many years to come, and when you do, I will not be able to help you."

Neza returned her gaze calmly. "I know," he said. "I have seen my death."

Xihu stared at him; a cold shiver ran through his body. He had little doubt that Neza was speaking the truth. But he felt a deep sorrow in his heart when he heard his young friend speak so quietly and certainly about his death.

The old woman nodded, and they sat for a long while in the light of the moon as it rose slowly and steadily to its zenith in the night sky.

Neza left the Temple City at the time of the autumn full moon. He sat with Xihu the last evening before his departure. "Come with me, old friend," he pleaded. "I need your wisdom and your patience. I am still young, and my fervor to change things at times outweighs my understanding of how much change people can accept."

Xihu looked at him for a long time. His heart longed very much to go with his radiant young prince, yet his mind whispered and was afraid to leave the Sacred City that had been his home for so many years. Here was all that was safe and known. He was one of the older priests, and was respected and acknowledged.

He sighed, "I am too old now to go with you, my prince. You need the young and the strong to build your kingdom. You need beautiful, young women to bear you sons, and nobles to give you stature, and warriors to give you power. You do not need an old priest with aching bones."

Neza reached out and covered his thin fingers with warm strong hands. "I wish you would come with me now. But will you promise to come to me if I ever have need of you?"

Xihu shivered as if a cold wind were blowing from the valley. There was an echo in Neza's voice of the night when he had spoken of his death.

"If you ever truly have need of me, my prince, I will come to you to the end of the world."

"I won't be that far away." Neza's teasing voice broke the chill in Xihu's heart. "I will be just a few days journey to the north. But if you get a message from me speaking of the White Temple, come quickly."

Months turned into years. Xihu heard many stories of the young prince who had taken back his father's kingdom and that his people had rejoiced. In the first years, he was lauded as a good and kingly ruler who re-established order in the kingdom and increased the power and the wealth of his people. He joined forces with other kings to re-establish peace in the country, and together they held off the invaders that so often had taken and destroyed their lands in the past. He built a summer palace on one of the mountains above the valley and there created gardens that became famous for their beauty, and the multitude of strange and exotic flowers and birds. He invited poets and musicians and priests from southern countries to spend the hot summers in his palace, where fresh mountain water ran in stone channels into large carved baths. All these things Xihu heard, and more.

At regular intervals, messengers came inviting him to visit the king at his palace, and once, the king himself came to see him. The youth whom Xihu had known had grown into a powerful man. His face had been molded into strong features, and his eyes were those of a man who often looked into far distances.

He stayed with Xihu for a few days, speaking of the changes in the laws he had made, telling him with laughter in his eyes of the sons and daughters, strong and beautiful, born to him by the women of his court; sharing with him the joy in his beloved, the one woman who had truly captured his heart. He pleaded again with Xihu to come with him and live with him in his royal city, but again, the fear of the unknown, of the crowds and the glamour, of the competition and struggles over power and influence in a royal city, and the fear of giving up his peaceful life of study and meditation held Xihu back.

The king had taken his hands and had held them for a long time before he left. "I wish you had been with me these years, my friend. There are others with me you would have come to love and cherish, and we could have had a rich life together. But you have chosen otherwise this time." He had left, and Xihu's heart had ached suddenly, and his chest had felt so heavy that he could hardly breathe.

Then came rumors that the king had become a heretic and had left the old gods in favor of a new one, a god without a face, the only, the invisible god Ipalnemohuani, "the One in whom we live." And Xihu was afraid. He knew Neza well enough to know that he was not a heretic. He thought he understood his longing to cherish the one perfect unifying force of creation in the universe rather than the endless variety and multitude of their present gods.

But he knew the people and their fear of anything that changed their lives much better than Neza, who had never been afraid of anything and for whom change was the breath of life. And he knew that any misfortunes befalling the land would be blamed on Neza abandoning the old gods.

The good years were followed by two years of drought, and the harvests were not enough to feed all the people. There were rumors that human sacrifices were held again to appease the angry gods, and that the people were afraid.

It was in the early summer of the following year that a runner came to the Sacred City, dressed in the colors of Neza's court and close to collapse with exhaustion.

He asked for Xihu and had to repeat his message to him three times until Xihu could hear it through the whistling of his breath. "The White Temple is falling. Come to the gardens quickly."

Xihu tried to ask him for more information, but the runner shook his head and would say no more. Xihu went to the high priest to ask for leave from the Sacred City and the use of some servants to carry a litter.

The old man looked at him sharply. "Where are you thinking of going, Xihu?" he demanded. "Does your journey have anything to do with the trouble your former charge has been creating for himself?"

Xihu shook his head. "No, High One," he lied steadfastly. "My sister is old and dying and has asked for my presence to ease her journey to the other world. But she sent word to hurry, for her body is frail and her soul barely attached to it."

"Well, then, journey in safety and guide your sister's soul into the world of the gods." The high priest still stared at Xihu as if trying to read his thoughts, but Xihu bowed deeply and retreated quickly to his quarters to pack a few provisions and some traveling clothes.

The litter carriers traveled swiftly, but it took them four days to reach the mountain where the king had his summer residence. The road leading up to the mountain was heavily guarded, and Xihu had to wait for a long time until a runner was sent to the king's quarters at the top of the mountain to announce his arrival.

He found Neza sitting in his bath, carved into natural rock overlooking the gardens. When he saw the old man approaching, Neza rose swiftly from the water and embraced the old priest. "I thank you for coming, my friend," he said, and there was a great joy in his voice.

Xihu sat heavily on the edge of the bath and looked out over the terraced gardens that cascaded over the hillsides. He turned to Neza sternly. "Why did you sent this messenger in such a hurry that the poor man nearly died from exhaustion? You seem in no distress or danger here."

Neza laid his arm around Xihu's shoulder. "My friend," he said quietly, "it looks peaceful here now, but it won't much longer. There has been a rebellion of my army in the capital. The rains have not come for two years, and the people are afraid, because they believe that the old gods are angry. I have refused to let them make sacrifices, and I have not gone and conquered other nations and made slaves and taken treasures from them. In the past years, I have written new laws and poems and songs. I have grown flowers and built a white temple in honor of the one, invisible God. And now, my people have grown tired of their peaceful king."

"But if you know of this rebellion, why do you not capture and execute the guilty? Or leave here and find a place where you can grow new gardens and honor your God?"

Neza smiled sadly. "I would betray all that I have tried to stand for if I killed men who are honest in their belief that I am not serving my people well. And I cannot run from here, because I am the king of my people. I have tried to bring them a new teaching and a new future. They were afraid of change, and now the future will come upon them with changes much greater and with such cruelty as none of them has ever dreamed."

Xihu stared at him in fear. "What are you speaking of, Neza?" he whispered. "What changes are you speaking of?"

"There will come a new people to this world, not in your generation and not in mine, but soon after, who will bring to an end all that my people and all other people of this our world have ever known. I wanted to bring them the God of Unity and Light. These new people also once knew of him, this God of Light, but they have corrupted his teachings in the image of their own greed. Now they will bring a god who will order the destruction of all of our old gods by force and they will build their own temples on the ruins of our temples. But you and I will not be here to see that day."

He turned and took a towel from the stone bench behind him. "Come," he said briskly. "Come and share a meal with me. I have asked you here because there is one treasure that I will not have fall in the hands of my enemies."

"A treasure?" Xihu stared at him. "But you were never one to worry about treasures or precious stones. What treasure is this that is so dear to your heart?"

Neza smiled. "Come and you will see." He climbed down the steep narrow stone steps carved into the rocks behind his bath. He led Xihu into a house with terraces opening wide to the gardens below, with the valley stretching far into the distance. At his entrance, a woman rose to great them. She was tall, though she only reached to Neza's chin. Her black hair shimmered and flowed unfettered over her shoulders. Her breasts were full and firm, and the golden jewelry adorning her neck seemed a natural part of her beauty.

"Xihu, this is my beloved, Xochil, who refuses to leave me in this time of danger. And as I love her more than my own life, I cannot force her to leave me. But she has consented to send with you our firstborn son." He turned to a small pallet in the corner where a child of no more than six months was sleeping, his little fists tightly closed by his cheeks.

"Oh my prince, how can you ask me to take your child from you?" Xihu said despairingly.

"How can I not? He will be safe with you, and you will teach him and love him as you have taught and loved me. If I should die now, there will be battles and turmoil and political intrigues. He will not be king after me. That is not his destiny. There is no other person I would trust more to give my own son to raise. We will send a woman with you who will nurse him and will take care of him as long he is in need of a woman's care. She has been Xochil's servant for years and can be trusted to keep the knowledge of his identity safe. But you will have to leave today. I have had word that the chiefs of my army have gathered in my capital and are on their way here. In a dream, I saw you taking the child with you, and my dreams have never betrayed me."

"I will tell the Old One that he is my sister's daughter's son, whom she was raising." Xihu's practical mind asserted himself, and Neza nodded his assent with a smile that reflected his love for his old teacher and his relief in knowing his child was in safe hands.

"He will be a good grandson to you, my friend," Neza's eyes twinkled, and then more seriously, he said. "Do not tell him about his father and mother until he is old enough to guard his secret. And when he is twelve, have him sent to the Temple in the south, to the Guardian of the Tomb. There, he will be given the knowledge he will need. They will teach him what I have tried to bring to my people here." He took from his neck the leather thong with the carved obsidian, which had been given to him by the priest in the southern temple. "Keep this for him. It will testify to his parentage."

He turned quickly and embraced the old man. Xochil stepped close to them and held Xihu's hands. "Take care of my little son," she whispered, and her eyes were shining with unshed tears. "His name is Xiantiouh."

At dusk, Xihu, the woman carrying the child, and the litter bearers descended the wide stone steps leading down from the mountain. Neza had insisted that they depart at once and not wait until the next morning. It was becoming hard to see when the woman, walking steadily on the steep steps, cradling the child in her arms, stopped.

"Listen," she whispered, "oh all the gods, listen. We have gone too late. They are coming up the mountain."

Xihu stared into the growing dark. He could see at the foot of the mountain a large gathering of torches smoking in the cool evening air and a multitude of people moving and murmuring like a flood.

"Quickly," the woman pointed, "quickly, in here. There is a cave here. It looks very small from the outside, and it is so far from the palace, maybe they will not search here."

She pushed Xihu toward the cave entrance. He had to crouch low to be able to enter. It was pitch dark in the cave, and dank and cold. The woman's whisper behind him was urgent.

"Feel your way to the left. There is an opening to another space large enough for all of us. And even if they shine their torches into the entrance, they won't see it unless they enter all the way."

They could hear the sounds of the people coming up the mountain like the wind rushing over the land before a thunderstorm.

And Xihu thought with sorrow that this storm would extinguish the one light that had burned brightly in the darkness for the people of his time. And he took the child from the woman and held him close to his heart, and he wept.

* * *

The angel looked at the soul before him and sighed a little. "Welcome back, old friend," he said, and Xihu gazed at the angel and sighed also.

"I am slow in learning," he said quietly, and the angel nodded.

"Yes, indeed. You keep missing opportunity after opportunity in your need for safety and your tendency to withdraw. You could have done much in helping Neza to move more slowly in the changes he made in his people's religious beliefs, showing him that although his knowledge was true, people were not ready for it and would be confused and frightened by it. And as for yourself, you could have learned much about taking more responsibility and working together with others."

"I have so many times regretted deeply that I did not do so," Xihu sighed again. "When I returned to my temple, life was so empty and meaningless, and I sorrowed for years about Neza's death. Raising his son seemed such a small thing I could do in return for him."

"It was not a small thing," the angel said consolingly. "You kept him in safety and gave him much love. You taught him well and were willing to let him go when it was time for him to go to the temples in the South. You did well in that."

"But if his father had lived, his son's life would have been so much different. He could have been king and ruled his people in wisdom and helped bring Neza's teaching to fruition!" Xihu exclaimed.

"It was not his destiny to become a ruler in this life," the angel responded and Xihu looked at him in amazement. "But how not, as the favorite son of a king?"

The angel shook his head. "Before you are born, you choose a certain role or task for yourself, one that will give you the best opportunity to learn the lessons for that life. Neza's son had chosen to gather knowledge and wisdom in this life, which he would then be able to use in his next life. To be a king, having to deal with all the struggles and responsibilities that such a role entails would have made it impossible for him."

"But why then did he choose to be born to a king?" Xihu wondered aloud.

"The body of each parent carries certain qualities that contribute to the bodies of their children similar qualities. Think of Neza, his curiosity and thirst for knowledge, his longing to understand eternal truth. All these are qualities that his son also had and they were essential to his learning in this life. His soul knew that he would not be able to spend much time with his parents. In a way, you were his parent as much if not more than his natural father and mother."

"Is that so for other children who do not grow up with their own parents?" Xihu asked.

"Often it is," the angel replied. "They choose their natural parents for the qualities of their bodies, but their other parents because of the quality of their lives with them, or because they have old connections that draw them together."

"Did I have such a relationship with Neza's son?"

"You, Neza, and all those close to him have been together in many lives and have shared many different relationships, and will do so again and again. You all agreed many lives ago that, as often as possible, you would come into incarnation as a group and use the energy of your group for the benefit of humankind. You have done so in the past and will do so again in the future. At times your individual destiny may take you to separate lives, but in the long run, you will always be reunited and work within this group."

"I am glad you told me this," Xihu smiled. "It makes the failures of this life easier to bear when I know I will have a chance to redeem them in the future."

"A chance!" the angel laughed, "My dear friend, there is no getting away from it, even if you wanted to!" and together they

walked down a path towards a courtyard where a large gathering
of people appeared to be involved in intense discussion, cheerfully
waving as Xihu approached.

"Welcome back, old man," one of them called out. "Ready for
the next round?"

And Xihu, knowing them all, joined them, his heart
overflowing with joy and gratitude.

CHAPTER SEVEN

The Temple

The young woman entered the temple courtyard where rows upon rows of pillars reached high into the sky, creating the illusion of a forest stretching far beyond vision. The ground was covered with fine gray sand, but in some areas large slabs, perfectly fitted together, were silent witnesses to the skill of the ancient artisans who had created the temples. She studied the hieroglyphs on the pillar next to her. They stood forth well defined by the brilliant sunlight, and it felt as if she could remember their meaning if she could just reach that secret place of knowledge deep inside her.

She could see her son moving among the pillars at the end of the temple. His hair shone brightly like a beacon when he moved from shadow into sunlight and she smiled. He had found this trip to be a great adventure—the journey on the river, the majesty of the ancient temples and tombs, the rides on camels and horses had awakened his curiosity, and he had asked her endless questions about the history of the places they were visiting.

She, five of her friends, and the three children had journeyed three days and nights on the river and had spent the evenings watching the sun sink into the ancient waters. They had seen children leading water buffaloes to drink on the river shores and donkeys moving in never ceasing circles around wells to pump up the water. It seemed that time had stood still here.

During the nights the ship had anchored in small towns, and they had entered a world that was full of strange and exciting sounds and smells. The two blond boys and the little girl had attracted much attention in the villages where foreigners and their children were rarely seen. The women, especially, had tugged and pointed and giggled and had been delighted when they could hold the little girl.

In some villages the people had remained remote, looking askance at the foreigners traveling through. Their children had stood silently by the doors staring, some little ones sitting and playing in the dust, oblivious of the flies covering their faces and clustering around their eyes.

The young woman had watched these children with compassion, and the doctor in her had protested when she saw how many of them were already blind in one eye or both.

They had seen the land rich and fertile on both sides of the great river, yet from the airplane, it had been clear how narrow the strip of fertile land really was. She had marveled at the courage and skill of a people that had for millennia brought forth food for its millions from such limited resource.

She had been amazed at the state of preservation of many of the ancient sites they had visited, and yet something had disturbed her. The temples and palaces had been empty, filled with dust and ancient echoes, and something in her had mourned. Sometimes she thought she could see the ancient life filling the temples and their courtyards—throngs of people dressed in simple white tunics or elaborate ceremonial clothes. But in the end, only the ancient high walls, the dust on the ground, the rapid voice of the guides had remained real.

She stood up and slowly began to walk among the pillars. She entered the wider path leading through the center and moved out into the open courtyard. She could see the large pool at the end of the path and the white obelisk gleaming in the sun.

"That does not belong here," she thought with sudden surprise. "There was nothing between the temple of the pillars and the pool . . ."

*   *   *

Egypt, circa 1000 BC

Netha walked silently behind her father, keeping her eyes on the back of his tunic. The guardians at the temple entrance had pointed westward towards the temple of the high pillars and had told them to follow the road leading beyond it to the smaller temple of Isis.

Her father was walking with measured steps; the servants, carrying her belongings and the gifts for the temple, followed him and Netha at a respectful distance. She tried to keep her eyes demurely lowered as would be seemly on this occasion, but her curiosity won over time and again, and she stole glances as often as she dared at her new surroundings.

She had been in temples before on occasions of high festivals and to bring gifts to the priests. But none of them had been as magnificent and awe inspiring as these.

She passed a group of young men dressed in the robes of acolytes, standing quietly together and talking to each other in lowered voices. Not one of them appeared to pay her any attention as she passed, and part of her was hurt. She had passed her twelfth year and her body gave clear evidence of the womanhood she had entered into only this year at the time of the river's rising. But then she remembered that she was not coming to the temple as a woman but as a disciple of the mysteries of Isis.

After the fever that had befallen her in her seventh year, she had been troubled for weeks by dreams that woke her in the middle of the night, and she would be bathed in sweat and cry inconsolably. Her parents had called the healer priest, and he had taken her with him to the healing room of his small temple and there sat with her while she slept. When she would wake from her dreams, he had held her hand and asked her in his gentle voice to tell him her dreams, and she had felt safer with him than she had ever with her parents: her pretty, small mother, round breasted and with full hips who spent hours painting her eyes and chatting with her women friends; her father, sturdy and broad shouldered, and forever spending time with his scribes keeping accounts of the tithes that he collected from the other landowners for Pharaoh.

The priest had listened to her dreams carefully for several nights and then returned with her to her parents. He had met with her father for a long time and in the end had called her into the room, where both men sat with serious faces among the papyrus of her father's scribes. The priest had said that her father had agreed to let her enter the temple of Isis when she had reached womanhood, and that until then, she would come to him for instruction and training to prepare her.

Netha had been afraid then, because she did not know what this meant. All the girls she had known to grow to womanhood were given in marriage to a man and then began to have babies. She knew of no girl who had to leave her home and receive instructions in a temple.

"Am I then not to marry when I grow up, and have children like other girls?" she finally had dared to ask with trembling lips. And Isthnahter, the priest, had taken her small hands into his slim long ones and held them gently like she had seen him hold an injured bird once in the temple.

"You have been chosen by the gods for different tasks in this life. Your dreams are a sign that your soul remembers this. You will find great joy and contentment in fulfilling these tasks when you grow into womanhood, little Netha. Many women can create new bodies for our souls as we return to earth again and again for learning. But only a few can learn the disciplines of the temples. We need those who can bring to the world the knowledge necessary for each generation to fulfill its true task on the long journey toward divinity. Your dreams have shown me that you may be such a one."

And then suddenly his serious face had brightened into a compassionate smile, and he had released her hands and turned her by her shoulders. "But now, little girl, run outside and play, for the wind is blowing from the river, and the water in your father's lily pond is cool and pleasant, and the blue dragonflies are waiting for you. Come to me in seven days' time, and I will show you pictures and tell you some stories that will be fun to listen to."

And she had run from the room, glad to get away from the serious men and the words she could not quite understand, except that her life was to be different from that of everybody else, and she was a little afraid.

But then she had begun to visit the temple and would spend the morning hours in the shady courtyard of Isthnahter's temple, and she had begun to cherish those hours. Over the years, he had taught her the meaning of hieroglyphs and how to decipher papyrus, which told stories about the gods. In her tenth year, he also began to teach her the beginnings of the healing arts and showed her how to recognize herbs and grasses, and she had learned their use in healing. He taught her a little about the inner structures of the human body and its workings, and Netha took delight in this learning. She began to appreciate the uniqueness that her visits to the temple gave her in the eyes of her peers, and it made up for the times when she saw the other girls sit together and dream and giggle and watch the young men of the estate pursue the older girls.

Isthnahter had also begun to teach her the skill of remembering and recording her dreams, and they would spend hours exploring the meanings of the dreams she recalled most clearly. She had begun to understand that people lived during the day in their heavy earth bodies, but at night when their bodies slept, they could move freely in their bodies of light, and travel swiftly and, depending on their desires and their training, move in the different realms of the inner worlds.

When the change of womanhood came to Netha, she was proud and excited, but at the same time she sorrowed, because she knew that her time of learning with Isthnahter was coming to an end. She had come to love the quiet, gentle healer. He knew her so much better than her parents who had slowly withdrawn from her and given their love and attention to the sisters and brothers who had been born after her, healthy, noisy and normal children with no dreams to disturb their nights.

And now she was walking behind her father who was bringing her to the temple of Isis to be examined, and if accepted, to be trained with the priests and priestesses of that temple.

They entered through a high gateway into a vast courtyard and, crossing it, entered into the cool darkness of the main temple. Two guards crossing spears hindered their entrance, asked for their destination in words of ritual and, bidding them to wait, resumed their station. A tall, young priest came from the darkness of the temple, and bowing slightly with his hands extended in greeting, led them to a small chamber to their right where he asked them to wait.

Netha was trembling. The silence of the temple, the massiveness of the temple walls, and the ceremonial questions of the guards inspired her with awe, and she thought with longing of Isthnahter sitting on the small stone bench in the little courtyard of his healing chambers, holding a scroll on his lap and teaching her patiently sign after sign, symbol after symbol. She thought of the smell of the herbs drying in the room where he mixed his medicines, and the warmth of the smooth stones in the courtyard long after the sun had set and the night wind blew cool from the desert.

An older priest entered, followed by two younger priests. Netha and her father rose and bowed deeply. The old man, his head cleanly shaved, greeted them courteously and took from her father the scroll with the message that Isthnahter had sent with her. He read it slowly and, lifting his eyes, which were the color of the evening sky, looked into her eyes with a gaze that Netha could not escape. She felt the rest of the world disappearing around her, and his eyes remained the only real thing she could cling to. They grew and grew until there was nothing in the world but these eyes and she felt she was falling, falling . . . .

She found herself sitting on the stone bench beside her father who held a strong, steady arm behind her shoulders, and Netha shivered, soaked in sweat like she used to be when waking from her dreams as a small child.

The priest was still looking at her, but now his gaze was gentle and he smiled, a smile that her reminded her a little of Isthnahter, and her fear began to subside.

"Come, little daughter, be welcome with us." He reached out with hands that were thin and old and brown like parched leather, but took hers with firmness and warmth. He nodded to her father. "Leave your gifts with the guardians here. We will safeguard them for your daughter until a final decision has been made as to her fitness for the teaching here. Then one-half will be given to the temple for her sustenance and the other will be given for the care of the poor and sick who come to the temple in search of healing."

He turned briskly and walked to the door. There he turned once more to address her father. "If your daughter passes the first rites and proves herself ready and willing to enter the final tests, she will return once more to your house to ponder her decision. If she chooses to enter the temple for life, she cannot return to you again. That is why we ask all students to search their hearts and souls to see if they are truly willing to give up the life of their families. Only a choice in full knowledge and freely made can bring the true dedication to their work here."

Something in Netha shrank into a small, trembling animal at his words, even though his voice had remained gentle and calm. To have to remain in these great, cold temples for the rest of her life, to give up all she had known and loved, all the people of her childhood, and with it also Isthnahter—it seemed a hard thing to ask.

The old priest turned to her and smiled: "It will be a long while till you have to make that choice, little girl. And then you will know better if it is worth making. Come now with me and let me show you the place where the young women of our school live, and meet some of them and the teachers who will instruct you."

Netha rose, troubled that he should have known her thoughts so clearly. She turned and bowed to her father, a formal little bow, and then suddenly she threw her arms around his neck and clung to him for a brief moment. She felt the tears welling in her eyes, and her throat felt as if she could not swallow. Her father stood stiffly, but when she released him, he took her face into his hands and looked into her eyes.

"May the gods be with you, child, and guide your road and lead you to wisdom. Bring honor to my house, and may honor be attached to your name always."

He turned abruptly and left the room, followed by the two younger priests, who escorted him through the courtyard and to the main entrance of the Temple City.

The old priest turned to Netha. "My name is Anathor. We all leave behind the names we were given as children, and we are given new names when we serve the gods. In the end, when you pass the final tests, you will know your real name, the one your soul was given at the beginning of time, the name that is your soul's very essence. It is the name that no one knows but you and He who created all living things, and the priest who will be your teacher of the mysteries. That name is never spoken by you or anyone except those I just named and then only during the Holy

Rites. But for now, you are still Netha until we chose a name of learning for you."

He led her out of the small, cool, dark room into the wide, sunlit courtyard and through another high stone gate into a smaller courtyard surrounded by white slim pillars. In the shadows a number of young women sat or walked, some little older than Netha, some fully grown, and two or three older women with graying hair. Anathor quickly crossed the space and led Netha to one of the older women who sat on pillows in the shade of a pillar. At their approach, she smiled up at them and rose. She was tall and stately, and her hair was long and dark and braided in patterns unfamiliar to Netha.

"This is Ishtar, a teacher from the East who has been with us for many seasons. She will show you your quarters and instruct you in your daily tasks and the times of your teaching. She will also be the person you can turn to with all questions and with any needs you may have."

Ishtar turned to Netha and laid her arm around her shoulders. "Come, little sister. You look weary and a little awed by our grand halls and temples. They soon will be home to you as your father's house was, and you will find as good friends here as you may have left behind."

Netha shook her head sadly. "There really was only one," she whispered, and tears rolled slowly over her cheeks. "Only one, and he was my teacher."

"Then you will find that here you can share with many more what you may have shared with him alone because those of your own age would not have understood. We all have had times of loneliness and felt like strangers in our parents' houses because we were different and had strange dreams and thoughts that others could not understand. You will see."

Netha wiped her face and smiled up at her. "It would be nice not to be so alone anymore," she said slowly, and then followed Ishtar into the shadow of the walkway that circled the yard and led into a room spacious and clean and cool, where she was given a bed and a chest to put her belongings in. There were three other beds in the room, though none of her future roommates were present.

Ishtar let her unpack her few belongings and then took her along to show her the baths, the kitchen, the rooms where the meals were taken, the gardens and pools, and the medicinal gardens where a profusion of herbs, grasses, and berries were growing, some immediately familiar, some so strange that Netha felt awe at the great variety of nature.

They continued to the hall leading to the inner temple of Isis, and Ishtar bade her sit on a small bench. She entered the darkness of the temple while Netha waited. She watched the sun patterns moving slowly over the stone slabs on the floor and the dust motes dancing in the sunlight. She listened to the chirping of the sparrows nesting in the small openings high up in the walls of the hall and to the voices of people talking and laughing in the gardens and courtyards outside, and then she fell asleep, exhausted from the journey, the excitement of her new surroundings, and the sadness of losing her only real friend. She slept deeply, slumped against the stone wall, her hands limply in her lap.

Ishtar returned with a young priest dressed in the robes of the Isis temple and looked at her with compassion.

"It is never easy for them," she said gently, "to let go of the familiar, and yet they belong here with us if they are to have any chance of fulfilling the tasks they chose for this life."

The young priest watched Netha's face closely. "Is she the one Isthnahter wrote us about?"

Ishtar nodded. "She started to dream early and the dreams frightened her and her family, so they brought her to the temple. I am glad he chose to become the healer there. Otherwise, some fool might have killed her with magic potions and medicines. She did not understand her dreams, but Isthnahter thought that they were visions of the future that she saw. It must have been hard for such a little girl to see some of the things the future holds. We may have to protect her from her full power for yet awhile."

She bent and touched Netha's face lightly. "Wake, little friend," she said, and Netha opened her eyes, bewildered by the strange surroundings.

The young priest sat down beside her and smiled. "Welcome to the house of the goddess, little sister. May your time with us be rich and joyful. May the goddess hold her hands over you and bring your soul into full flowering. May you find fulfillment of your life's longing and your spirit's journey." He bent forward and traced a sign on Netha's forehead. "You are to be given a new name as you join our temple, and I have searched for one that would fit the shining of your soul. So your temple name with us will be Kihra. May it recall to you your timeless self whenever you hear it."

She smiled shyly at him, liking his kind face and gentle voice. He, too, reminded her of Isthnahter, and she suddenly felt less alone and not so far from home.

That night she slept deeply and dreamlessly in the room with the other three young women. Two were older than she and had been at the temple for many moons. The third, a small, very skinny girl with large brown eyes and tightly curled hair, had only come to the temple a moon ago, and again Netha felt less alone, knowing she was not the only recent newcomer.

The next year Netha spent in an intense process of learning and training. She rose at dawn and, after an early meditation in the temple, attended classes until midmorning, when she broke fast with the other students. She worked in the gardens until the midday break, when the girls were allowed to rest or swim in the large pools. Afternoon classes continued until sundown and were concluded with another evening meditation in the temple before the evening meal.

The days were full and rich, and Netha enjoyed learning and the fellowship with her teachers and companions. She began to share her thoughts and knowledge with the others and found that

Isthnahter had prepared her well for her entrance into the temple. She found she was ahead of her peers in the knowledge of hieroglyphs, medicinal herbs, and healing arts. Yet she began also to realize that greater knowledge was still waiting to be discovered.

She learned new skills: the control of her body's rhythms, the trance states that allowed her to leave her body and, in full awareness, travel free of her body to places she knew. Yet she was always instructed by her teacher where to go and what to observe, and when she once tried to go to the places of her childhood, she was recalled sharply, and for the first time reprimanded.

"The skills you are taught here are not for your own use but are for the service of others. Only in extreme need are we permitted to use them for ourselves. Not for pleasure or curiosity or to demonstrate our powers to others." Her teacher's voice was firm, and Netha hung her head. She had so longed to see her teacher again, yet she knew that it had been for her own need that she had wanted to see him.

At the end of her first year, her teachers tested her newly learned skills, and Netha knew that they were satisfied with her progress. In the second year she began instructions with Anathor and Ishtar and other new teachers in learning about the culture, history, and philosophies of other peoples. She was shown maps of the lands surrounding the great river and the lands across the inner sea, and learned of the history of the lands that had existed before the great floods. She learned the names of stars and constellations and the influences they were known to have over the fate of people and whole nations. She learned about the history of the Temple of Isis and of the tasks that the priests and priestesses had assumed centuries ago—to preserve the wisdom from ages past and to be the guardians over this wisdom as it was used to help mankind in its slow journey into the future.

For three years more, Netha studied and grew in spirit and body. The memory of her family and her home became dim. But her memory of Isthnather never dimmed in her heart and her mind. She found herself dreaming of him often and felt shy about recording these dreams, as she had learned to record all her other dreams. She cherished these dream memories of sitting with him in the small temple, reading or talking or working in the small herb gardens, as much as her real memories, and often wondered if she truly had gone in her night body to be with him. After her first rebuke not to use her new training for her own ends, she had never attempted to do so again. But she felt that her dreams were gifts, not sought but given to her. She did not examine the fact that she wanted to keep them secret, but she felt a sense of guilt over it.

At the end of her fourth year, Netha was called to meet with Anathor and Ishtar. She sat quietly as they reviewed with her the progress she had made. They outlined the future tasks she was to learn in preparation for her final tests before entering the priesthood. Then Anathor leaned forward, peering at Netha intently.

"There is knowledge that bestows power on the knower—power far beyond what we could ever learn in a lifetime on our own. To safeguard this power, we have to become unselfish, to free ourselves of those needs of the body, the emotions, and the mind that would tempt us to misuse these powers for our own ends. For this power may only be used safely in the service of the greater good, in the service of the forward going of mankind, never for the needs of the one or the few. Our lives here prepare us for this service. The training you have received here has been demanding, and living so closely with others serves well to reveal any flaws or traits in a person that could lead to such a corruption of power."

"You have learned easily and shared freely of your knowledge, Kihra. I have seen no small mindedness in your being, no greediness, envy, or need for power. You are holding back a small part of yourself, and only you know what that is. Your time is coming to return to the home of your family. You will spend three months there. Search your heart and your mind to determine whether you are truly willing to return to us here for the rest of your life and give all that you are and can become to the service that we have taken upon ourselves here—to be the guardians of the old wisdom and add to it what our heart and mind and spirit reveal to us in our own lifetimes. Go back to your old life and search your heart well. If there are any reservations, face them truthfully. Only if we are true within ourselves can we become free. Only if we are free can we serve others freely. Our blessings are with you, younger sister, and our hopes for your joyful return."

Netha rose, bowed, and left the chamber. She had no wish to return to her family. The only person she longed to see was Isthnahter. Yet she realized the wisdom of the practice of sending the students back into the world of their past, to let them experience one more time the pleasures and pains of the life of the other world. Only thus could they choose the life of service in the temple consciously and in full knowledge.

She returned to her home, accompanied by two temple guards. Her father, grown much older, greeted her with formality and respect, finding it difficult to see in the tall, self-contained young woman the lively child he had left in the temple four years ago. Her mother greeted her with kisses and tears, and Netha returned her greetings kindly. She felt no kinship to her, who had also aged greatly and tried with more artifice to cover the signs of increasing age. Two of her sisters had married and left the house. Her younger brother was visiting her father's brother at Pharaoh's court, and the older one had taken a guest of her father on a lion hunt. Her youngest sister, Rethi, an awkward, gangly child of ten with beautiful brown eyes, greeted her sister shyly and was clearly in awe of her, and Netha felt her heart go out to this child who seemed to be as alone as she herself had always felt.

She rested briefly from her journey and then asked her father about the well being of Isthnahter. Her father stared at her, frowning. "The old priest? They said he became ill a year after you left, too ill to be any use as a healer here. So he returned to the temple of the goddess. Did you not know? I thought he belonged to the Temple of Isis. Did you not meet him there?"

Netha stared at him. "No," she finally whispered. "He never returned there. They would have told me. He would have asked for me." Her eyes filled with tears, but she was ashamed to let her father see them. She rose in haste. "I will walk in the gardens for a while," she said, "I trust they are still as beautiful and peaceful as they used to be."

Her father watched her out of the corner of his eyes. "Peaceful enough," he grumbled. "Your sister and the gardener are the only ones to walk in them. I wonder why I bother to keep them up." He turned abruptly and picked up a scroll.

Netha hurried through the garden, barely glancing at the flowers she used to love so much and left by the small side gate. She hurried along the footpath that led near the river to the temple. She entered the temple's courtyard but it was deserted of human life. There was dust and refuse everywhere, and the small pool in the courtyard was dry and filled with rotting leaves. The sounds of someone working in the gardens led her outside. An old man was hoeing the dry soil, lifting out dead plants. Netha did not recognize him. "I have come to find the priest of the temple," she said.

The old man peered at her with inflamed eyes. "There has been none here these past two years. After the old one left, they sent a young one. But he did not last long. Wanted too many gifts for his healing, so folks did not ask him for help. And those that did, it didn't do them much good. He was no healer like the old one. It was a shame that the old one had to sicken and leave us."

Netha bent her head. "Do you know where the old priest went from here?" The old man shook his head. "No, he did not say. Only said he was going home. I thought he meant his old temple, but I don't know where that might be." His leathery old face suddenly became alert. "Did you know him well? Is that why you come asking like this?"

Netha nodded. "Yes, he was my teacher for a while."

The old man suddenly straightened and bowed. "Forgive me, Holy One, I did not know your were of the priesthood. My eyes are not as good as they used to be."

Netha had to smile. "Only a student, yet, old man; be at peace. But I longed to see him again."

"He left some things behind, some scrolls and pictures. Would you like to see them? I found them when I was cleaning the herb room and put them aside. The other one never bothered with the herbs. He only used prayers and magic."

"Yes, I will come and look," Netha sighed. The old man clearly wanted to help, and she did not want to disappoint his goodwill. They entered the herb room, and Netha looked with sadness at its dusty, empty tables and cabinets. The old man rummaged in a chest in the corner where Isthnahter had kept the scrolls describing the proper mixture of medicinal herbs and preparation of tinctures.

He lifted out two scrolls. "These are the ones I found by his bed. He was too ill to pack his own things, so they took him in a litter and maybe forgot them."

Netha took them gently from the old man's shaking hands. She carried them into the courtyard, for the sun was sinking into the west and the light in the small room was getting too dim to encipher the writing.

One scroll contained the ritual prayers of the service to Isis. The other carried her name on the seal. Netha broke it with trembling hands, tears dimming her eyes.

"Little friend, I am glad to know you are in safe hands now that will guide you with wisdom on the path that was preordained since your birth. I am grateful to have been here to help you find your road. My body has weakened greatly of late, with an old illness that has resumed its power. I will seek help with some friends who may find a way to make this old body last yet a while. But no matter. It has served me well. I have fulfilled most of my tasks for this lifetime. If more is asked of me, the gods will need to do their share to give me the strength. My love and my thoughts will be with you always on your journey. Serve her well, our Goddess of Light and Love, in whose care I have entrusted you. Do not grieve for me. The separation is only of the body. Our souls are always joined in freedom. Isthnahter."

Netha sank on the little stone bench where she had so often sat by his side. She held the scroll in her lap and stared at the setting sun. He had wanted her to know that he was dying. And she had gone on all these years thinking him alive and well. All her dreams, nothing but her own memories! Were, then, all her dreams just figments of her own imagination? Did any of the things she had learned mean anything? Were the ceremonies of the temple just empty rituals, perpetuated to give a reason for existence to the priests and priestesses there?

Despair was sinking like a dark cloud over her mind, and she could not think clearly. She rose.

The old man had watched her with concern. "Did you find what you were looking for?" His voice was hoarse from disuse.

She smiled at him with an effort. "Yes, I found it," she said and her mouth was so dry she had to repeat her words. "Come to my father's house in the morning. It is the great house with the palm grove, close to the river. He will reward you for your help."

"The tithe collector?" The old man looked at her in disbelief.

"Yes, the tithe collector. For once he will give, not take from you." She bent her head in greeting and turned away, and with a heavy heart began her journey home.

She found again the large rock where she had sat often with Isthnahter at night to watch the stars. She sat there for a long time while the stars wheeled in the sky and her tears flowed freely. She wondered how much longer Isthnahter had lived after he had left, and where he had died. She thought again about the vividness of her dreams and wondered why she had been given no indication that he no longer inhabited his earthly body. If hers had been true dreams, would he not have told her? She sat long on the smooth rock while the cool night wind tugged at her hair and dried her tears. She let her sorrow and the longing for him who had been the first, and maybe the only, person who truly knew and loved her fill her whole being.

When the moon rose in the east, she found her way home, the narrow path through the reeds clear in the moonlight and the river shimmering like another path of silver beside her.

She woke early in the morning from the noise of people running and shouting in the hallways of the house, and then her sister Rethi came into her room, stumbling in her haste. "Netha, please come, quickly. Father's guest, he was hurt in the hunt. They traveled all night to bring him here. He has been bleeding badly and now is in a fever. Please, Father asked me to get you to help. Mother is no use; she just shivers and cries. She can't stand the sight of blood and I have no skills."

Netha rose from her bed and dressed hurriedly. "Are there still healing herbs growing in the garden?" she asked Rethi.

The young girl nodded. "Inthet kept them after you left. He has been teaching me what he learned from you. He said somebody in the house should have some knowledge, and nobody else seemed to care much except Manatha, who helps with birthing the children."

Netha smiled and laid her hand on Rethi's hair. "I am glad, little sister, that you cared. Now run and find me two handful of silverweed, and rinse it well in clear water, and bring that to the room where they took the guest. Also have the servants bring fresh water from the well and clean linen to the room."

She left her room and, following the commotion in the house, found her father and brother bending over a makeshift stretcher. Netha joined them. The man on the stretcher was tossing restlessly and moaning. Although his eyes were open, he did not appear to recognize people around him. His clothes were torn and crusted with dried blood.

Netha bent down. "Help me get these clothes off him," she ordered briskly. She turned to her brother. "Tell me what happened to him and how long ago."

Her brother, frowning and with a voice that shook from exhaustion, tried to recollect himself. "We were at a distance of two days travel from here. We had killed one lion and N'athon went to make sure that he was dead when his mate attacked from behind a bush. N'athon fell when the lion jumped him, and he must have struck his head because he did not defend himself. When we killed the lion and pulled N'athon from underneath, he was not conscious, but he was bleeding heavily from the lion's mauling. But I wonder whether it is the injury to his head that has had him raving for two days. He lost much blood, but none of the injuries looked too deep. We traveled since then to bring him home." He sat down heavily, struggling to keep his eyes from closing.

"Go and rest, little brother," Netha said with compassion. "There is nothing you can do here now. You have done well to bring him back. He needs rest and care, and so do you." She turned back to her charge and with her father's help removed the last blood-soaked tatters from the powerfully built body. "Who is he, father?" she asked curiously as she began to wash dust and crusted blood from chest and shoulders.

"He is N'athon, an envoy to Pharaoh's court from the northern provinces. He came here to take a few days' rest and to hunt. Will he be well, daughter? It would bode ill for our house if Pharaoh's guest came to harm under my care." Her father peered anxiously at the man who had calmed under Netha's ministrations and now lay quietly, but still without awareness, on the bed where they had moved him.

"If the blow to his head is not too severe, he will do well. The other injuries are superficial, though some of them have started to fester. But they will heal in time. It is the head that concerns me. And only time will tell how much hurt has been done there." Netha took the herbs that Rethi had brought and applied them to the injuries. When she finally had finished bandaging the last wound, she sat back. "I will stay with him and hold watch," she said. "He may become restless again and may need calming. Bring me more fresh water and some food for myself. And you, Rethi, maybe can come once in a while to see if I need anything else. But most of all he will need quiet in a darkened room."

For three days Netha tended the stranger, becoming familiar with his face, which showed strength and courage even in the absence of consciousness, and his well-formed body that was beginning to heal from its wounds. On the fourth morning, she rose to find him awake and watching her with an amused smile.

"I do not know who you are, but I am pleased to find you in my room, beautiful goddess. I seem to remember your face, but I thought you were only part of my fevered dreams of the past days. Tell me who you are and I will build a temple to your honor."

Netha blushed and frowned at the same time. "I am the daughter of this house and have tended your injuries, as is my task as an apprentice healer of Isis." She reached for a cup of water and held it out to him. "You need to drink this and much more. You have lost much blood and suffered a severe blow to your head. You have been in a fever for five days. You need to rest and not talk too much."

His eyes smiled at her, though his face remained serious. "I will do as you order, goddess, but only if you stay here for a while."

"I will stay as long as your healing requires," Netha answered tartly, though she had to turn her head to hide her smile.

She attended to N'athon's needs for another week until he had regained his strength sufficiently to leave his room and to walk in the coolness of the gardens. He still suffered from recurring headaches, and once Netha found him sitting on a bench holding his head and staring blankly at the pond. When she called his name, he turned toward her and looked at her with something resembling fear.

"There are things I cannot remember," he whispered. "Why is that?"

"It happens often after injuries to the head," Netha reassured him. "Your memories will return in time." And she sat beside him, taking his hand into hers, filled with a strange emotion at seeing this powerful man helpless and at a loss.

He looked at her gratefully, and some of the old mockery came back into his voice. "Goddess, what would I have done without you?" He bent his head over her hand and kissed her fingertips.

Netha felt a sudden heat rising in her body and got up quickly. "Rest here in the shade for a while; it is hot. I will send you some drink," and she fled, her heart beating rapidly in her chest.

The weeks passed and Netha found herself more and more bewildered by her feelings for N'athon. They continued to spend much time together, and she showed him her favorite places on the river. He treated her with his mocking respect and asked her occasionally about her time in the temple. Netha found it difficult to speak about her training. Somehow those years had suddenly become remote to her, overshadowed by the reality and the urgency of caring for N'athon, being in his vibrant presence, feeling the warmth of his strong hand as they walked in the dusk by the river.

At the end of the second month of her time at home, they sat as they had many times before, on the large rock by the river, watching the sickle of the new moon shimmer in the evening sky. N'athon pulled her into his arms and held her close. "I will soon have to leave here to return to my country, Netha. Will you come with me and leave your temple for me?"

Netha felt the warmth of his body and the strong beat of his heart against hers. Her mind whirled. "I do not know," she whispered. "Give me time, please, give me more time."

He nodded and released her gently. She felt the immensity of the dark night enveloping her, leaving her alone in a cold, lonely emptiness, and she suddenly longed for the safety of his arms and his warm strength. She leaned against him. "Please," she whispered, "please hold me. I need to feel you close to me. I am so alone."

He took her into his arms again and laid her gently to the ground. He began to caress her face and his hands traveled over her body. She clung to him and let him explore her body until they both were consumed in the fire of passion and united their bodies in a rising wave of flame.

The morning sun found them still by the river. They had spent much of the night in an ever again rising hunger of their bodies, and Netha woke in the dawn, cold and sore and exhausted. N'athon was sleeping beside her, and she saw him suddenly as if for the first time. He had been tender with her in his first taking of her body, but later in the night had shown himself to be a man knowledgeable in the art of raising the body to passions that had begun to frighten her. Never before had she been a slave to her body's needs, and something in her rebelled at the thought of becoming imprisoned by them now.

She suddenly knew that she could not go with N'athon, no matter how passionately her body desired him. She longed for the quietness of the temples and the peace of the sacred rituals, the discipline of the work, and the simple and uncomplicated relationships with her teachers and peers.

She bent over N'athon and gently held his face. He woke quickly and took her hands. "Will you come with me, goddess? Do you know your heart's desire now?"

His eyes searched her face. She smiled at him with sadness and kissed his eyes. "I cannot," she said. "Part of me wants to be with you always, and my body desires the passions of yours. But I know now that we would not bring each other happiness. Our tasks are different for this life, and we cannot betray them without bringing great unhappiness to each other. I am grateful to have known you and loved you. Let me go in peace to my task. You will always be in my heart."

He stood up and took her into his arms. "May you find peace, little goddess. I thank you for your healing. And for giving yourself to me with all the richness and the fire of your being."

At the end of the third month, just before Netha was to return to the temple, she found that she was late in her monthly bleeding.

A sudden dread overcame her. Could it be that the one night of passion would have left her with child? She sent a message to the temple, claiming illness to delay her return. At the end of two more weeks, she had no doubt of her condition. Her heart and mind were in turmoil.

There was no strict demand of celibacy for the priests and priestesses of the temple, but those in training were required to abstain from the passions of the body, and she could not envision returning with a child to the temple of Isis. She feared the reaction of her parents and the dishonor that they would see in her condition. She found that she did not want to bear a child of N'athon, whom she would never see again.

She walked in the gardens restlessly, trying to control the growing nausea that the pregnancy began to induce in her. She was sitting in the shadow of a flowering bush, staring at the lotus blossoms in the pond and the dragonflies hovering over the water, when she looked up to meet the compassionate eyes of Manatha, the old woman who had served as a midwife on her father's estate for decades and had brought Netha herself into the world. The old woman sat down beside her on the stone bench and took her hands into her old, frail ones.

"I know what is troubling you, little one. I have watched you for days now and I know the signs. Is it such a bad thing to carry a child, even if the man who fathered it is not with you any longer? Is not any child a gift of the gods?"

Netha shook her head in despair, tears welling up at the gentleness of the old voice. "I cannot bear this child to fullness. I betrayed my task once already, and I cannot return to it if I bring this child into the world." She turned suddenly and stared at the old woman. "Are there not herbs that will drive forth the fruit of the womb before its time? You must know about these. There must be other women who found themselves with child at the wrong time of their life or felt they were too old and frail to carry a child to term. Please, old mother, please help me."

The old woman looked at her with troubled eyes. "If you truly do not want it, why not let it ripen in your body to give it to another woman who is barren? Although there are ways to free your body from it prematurely, you will carry a debt for returning it to the gods, a debt you will have to pay some other time."

"I will pay that debt gladly if only now I could go back to where I need to be."

Manatha rose. "I will make you a draught that will bring forth the unripe seed of your womb. There is a danger that you may bleed heavily if it tears itself free too forcefully."

"I take that risk," Netha whispered. "I need to be free to return to the temple."

That night the draught took effect, and Netha found herself in great pain, as her body was forced to interrupt a process that should have taken months to complete. She began to bleed, and in the morning found her strength ebbing. Manatha sat beside her bed in tears, holding her hands. She gave Netha another draft of herbs to stop the bleeding, but to no avail. Her mother came to her room with fearful eyes and left again. Netha fell into a light sleep between the waves of pain that continued to rack her body. She woke at dusk to the light of a small oil lamp by her bedside. Manatha sat in a small chair, asleep, her old wrinkled face marked by sorrow. Netha could feel the blood seeping from her body, but the pain had stopped. The door opened quietly and a tall stooped figure entered. It came into the light of the lamp and Netha could see the face.

"Isthnahter," she whispered with joy and disbelief, "am I, then, dead already that you come to take me with you?"

He took her cold hands into his, warm and firm and very real. His face, aged, was sad, and his eyes were filled with compassion. "No, little one, I am not dead. I was ill for a long time. But these last months, the goddess was gracious and gave me a reprieve. I went to the temple to inquire of you, and they told me you were at home to consider your decision. Anathor was troubled because you had delayed your return, and so was Ishtar. So I came to look for you myself. And now I find you on the doorstep of death. Could you not have trusted them to help you rather than do this violence to your body? There always is a space for a child to grow and learn in the temple. Yet always you had to keep part of yourself secret from others."

"You were gone and I thought you dead. There never was anybody else I loved and trusted as much as you. With you gone from my life, nobody else could fill your place."

Isthnahter held her face in his hands. "The others loved you too, if only you had let them come into your heart. That was the lesson you still had to learn. That they all were as close to you as you thought me alone to be."

"I know that now," she whispered, and than with a last upwelling of fear and despair, she asked, "Will you stay with me until the end?"

"There is no end, only a passing, little one. But I will stay by your side until you have passed safely over the threshold. Then you will be free and will need no more help from me."

She smiled weakly, holding tightly to his hand as she felt a cold numbness rising in her legs that made it impossible for her to move.

Isthnahter's eyes held hers, and they were pools of silver in the moonlight as the cold and the numbness rose up in her body until it reached her heart and stilled its frantic, fluttering beat. She rose from her body and floated above it. "Thank you for a safe passage, beloved friend," she whispered, and turned to follow the path to the river that lay shimmering in the moonlight.

*   *   *

"Oh my child," the angel said, and his voice was full of sorrow and compassion, "why did you feel you had to do this. There was so much to do and learn in this life! You had planned for this life so carefully, because of the opportunities it could give you."

"But that is why I could not have the child!" Netha cried out.

"Don't you understand? I thought I could not go back to the temple carrying a child!"

"Were there not other ways you could have solved that problem?" the angel asked. "It was not only the burden of bringing a child to the temple that brought you to this decision, was it?"

Netha was silent for a long time. "No," she finally admitted, "no, I was ashamed to let them see that I had succumbed to my passions. And I would also have had to admit that I felt so lost when I thought Isthnahter had died, and when I believed that all my dreams of him had been illusions or wishful thinking. It was this despair that drove me into N'athon's arms. No, much of it was my pride, my need to be perfect and my unwillingness to admit to my human failings."

"Yes," the angel nodded sadly, "I am glad you can see this now."

"What happened to the child?" Netha asked anxiously. "Is it here with you?"

The angel shook his head. "No. The soul of what would have been your child saw that you were not welcoming it and never entered the body it was preparing for itself. It will soon find another body and another family. Yet you have incurred a debt for interrupting a process that is one of the most creative aspect of life—the formation of a new body for a soul to enter into. This is not lightly done."

Netha looked at the angel anxiously. "What will I have to do to redeem this debt?"

"For some women, it may be that in another life they will be unable to conceive, or may be unable to carry a child to full term. You will choose to be born into a life where you will have none of the opportunities or talents you had in this one. You will be a very humble and simple woman, with few skills, yet you will have a child and this child will be the most important and precious part of your life, and you will give it everything you have, most of all your love. Thus you will learn humility and learn to love another more than yourself."

"Will I see Isthnahter again?" Netha asked timidly.

"Not in that life," the angel responded. "You will have to learn that lesson on your own. There will be other lives in the future when you will be working with him again, for you are bound to him and others by bonds of love and mutual agreements from the past.

"And the child?" Netha wondered.

"Any child that you bear is part of your past and your future," the angel replied. "It is drawn to you by bonds of love or because you both need to resolve old issues. Offering to build a body for a friend is a great gift you can give, as is providing a safe haven for the first years, when a child is helpless and needs much care. In its later years, you can offer learning and wisdom and, by the example of how you live your life, give much in preparing a child for its own life. Most people do not understand this. Many bodies are created primarily as the result of lust, with little understanding or caring about the soul that may want to enter the body that is being created. And so the souls that are attracted are often souls in the early stages of their journey, responding to the vibrations of the bodies of the parents. Some parents want children to perpetuate their family or dynasty, and will attract souls who respond to that energy. Other parents want children so that they have someone to take care of them when they become old. Few want children with the conscious understanding that it is a loving service they offer to a soul that wants to enter into another incarnation. You, if you had stopped to think, had that understanding, and could have offered such an opportunity. And as always, with greater understanding comes greater responsibility."

Netha bowed her head in quiet acceptance: "I know that what you say is the truth, and I should have known it, too. But are there not times when a woman conceives a child and it is not possible for her to take care of it? Would it not be better for the child not to be born rather than die later of starvation or suffer in other ways?"

"Sometimes that can happen, and then the debt of the woman who makes the decision not to carry the child to fullness is a lesser one. Yet often the decision is one of convenience, not of conscience."

"And what of women who have been forced by men and thus have conceived without consent?"

"That is always a sorrowful thing," the angel said softly, "because what should be an act of love and joyful creation becomes an act of violence and horror. There are no easy answers for these questions, child. Some day women will have the freedom to conceive children only when they are fully prepared to love them and care for them, but that time will not be for a long time to come."

"But now," said the angel, "let me take you to a place where you can ponder and rest for a while before you take on your next task." And putting his arm around her, he guided her to a beautiful garden where a small stone bench stood in the shade of an ancient willow tree and a lily pond was dreaming in the sun with dragonflies shimmering over the water.

CHAPTER EIGHT

Fire on the Mountain

The woman sat on the old oak log. An hour before, after an evening of exploring the plans for the new project they were all working on together in the city, one of her friends had stood up, stepped out on the terrace, looked at the clear night and the stars outside, and had declared: "Enough for tonight. Let's go out and make a bonfire." And everyone had eagerly dragged branches and broken-down chairs and lumber left over from the renovation of the house into the old shale pit.

In the end it had made quite a pile, and when they had lit the fire, it had roared up into the night sky with great eagerness. The sparks had risen in wide, golden spirals, alive like fireflies in a magic dance. Some of the younger people had leaped through the fire when it had begun to die down.

Now they all sat together quietly on rocks and logs and watched the fire burn. Some big logs were glowing in deep reds, and the fire had created golden caves with a flowing light that moved mysteriously in them.

The woman shifted her weight a little on the hard log. Her son, grown suddenly in one of the intense spurts of adolescence, was leaning against the old fir tree growing in the entrance to the pit. His face was quickly losing its childlikeness. He had been very quiet all night, and she wondered what he saw in the flames.

She stared into the fire. It had been eight years now since Ethan had died, after the year-long battle against the illness that had brought an end to their time together. Yet life had continued, and so had the work that they had shared with their friends for so many years. After the pain had subsided and the emptiness in her heart had become something she had gotten used to, there had emerged, slowly in the beginning like the tips of spring flowers, a little hope, first, and then a growing conviction that life would not just be endless, lonely drudgery, but could again be filled with richness and joy. And there was the sure knowledge that his life had given meaning to all of them far beyond his death. She remembered with a quick smile how he had loved fires and could sit in complete silence for hours looking into the flames.

A big branch, aglow with the red-golden light, collapsed on itself and another shower of sparks spiraled up into the night sky. The tree frogs were calling in the woods below the house, and the rich smell of moist earth drifted up the hillside.

Her friend with the dark beard and the bright blue eyes lifted a small drum to his knees and began to tap out a rhythm. It was an archaic sequence, slow and regular in the beginning and then picking up speed. The young woman sitting beside him, her hair shimmering like spun gold down to her waist, tapped the rhythm with her foot. "It is irresistible," she said softly and smiled. She stood up and began to turn, raising her arms and clapping her hands in the rhythm of the drum, slowly at first and then in ever increasing speed, her red, green, and blue striped skirt beginning to open like a flower, whirling in circles around and around, the flames blazing, and the drum beating . . . .

* * *

Asia, circa 1500 BC

Mirrha sat proudly by the largest of the fires. This was her feast. The tribe was celebrating the birth of her firstborn, the first son to their young chief and his young wife. Mirrha looked at the child, who was watching the fire with his dark eyes. He had been born three moons ago and the birth had been easy. But then Mirrha was strong and young, and she had known that she would have no trouble giving birth even to such a big child.

The women of the tribe were standing in a circle, ready to begin the traditional dance of celebration, and when the drummer began the rhythm they began to turn, slowly first, and then faster and faster, their sturdy brown feet stamping down the dusty grass of their gathering place, their hands echoing the rhythm of the drums, sharp and accompanied by the jingling of their bronze bracelets.

She could see the men sitting on the other side of the fire, solemnly watching the dance of the women, some of them nodding the rhythm with their heads. Arrhal sat in their midst, the fire lighting up his bronze-colored features and his blue-black hair, held in a long braid. He glanced across the fire and saw Mirrha watching him. He smiled and, rising in one swift motion, picked up one of the bowls they used to serve the honey drink. Stepping lightly, he came over to her and held the vessel to her lips. He laid his hand briefly on the head of the baby and caressed the thick black hair. "He will be a strong warrior for his tribe," he said smiling, and Mirrha's heart was so filled with a fierce joy that she felt it could contain no more.

The women tirelessly danced and danced; the beating of the drums and the stamping feet went on through the night. Sometime much later, when the moon had set and the valley wind started to blow cold over the dancing place, Arrhal came and picked her up where she had dozed off, tired from the excitement of the feast and the honey drink, and carried her and the baby to their tent. Mirrha, only half awakened, pulled the furs over the three of them and quickly sank back into a deep slumber, still filled with the rhythm of the drums and the stamping feet and the whirling fire.

Mirrha awoke in the middle of the night. At first she did not know what had awakened her. The moon threw sharp light and shadows through the half-opened flap of the tent. She could hear the baby snuffle quietly beside her. Turning toward him to see if he was covered, Mirrha saw that Arrhal was not in the tent. She rose quietly, so as not to disturb the child, and stepped toward the tent entrance. The light of the moon, nearly full, flooded the high plateau, and the shadows of the rocks and an occasional scrubby bush stood out in sharp contrast.

A movement on the sheep path leading toward the low mountain range that enclosed the plateau made Mirrha turn. She thought that she saw Arrhal's white sheep fur shining in the moon's light. But she could not understand why he was walking at what seemed a very fast pace toward the mountain. She shivered in the cold wind and turned back towards the tent to get her fur cloak.

At that moment, she saw the unmistakable silhouette of Yarhun, the tribe's shaman, step forth from his tent, set aside from the other yurts by custom. He approached quietly and laid a restraining hand on Mirrha's shoulder.

"Do not try to follow him," he whispered. "You may not follow him where he has to go tonight." Mirrha looked into the nearly luminous eyes of the old man, who was so thin that his skin seemed to cover nothing but bones and sinews, yet who was dressed in nothing but a small loincloth, his magic charms hanging in a small leather pouch around his neck.

She swallowed her fear of the old man and whispered back, "But where is he going in the middle of the night?"

The shaman looked at her for what seemed like an eternity.

He looked up to the moon, and then his gaze followed the now small figure of Arrhal, who had covered already nearly half the distance to the mountain.

"The gods have called him. He will be a great leader of men, and the gods will instruct him," the shaman said. His glance continued to follow Arrhal's disappearing figure. Mirrha suddenly felt his deep longing to go with Arrhal to the place where the gods would talk with him.

"How long will he be with the gods?" she asked timidly. "He took no food or water, and he has only the small cloak, and the nights are cold in the mountains."

The shaman looked at her suddenly with displeasure. "Go to your tent, woman," he said firmly, "and mind your child and your woman's business. When the gods choose to instruct a man, it is not the time to worry about food and water and small or large cloaks." And with this, he turned abruptly and strode back to his tent, his charms rattling in the leather pouch.

Mirrha stood by the tent entrance. She dared not do what she most wanted to do—gather some provisions and Arrhal's large black fur cover and ride after him. She knew that if she rode very fast, she even now could catch up with him before he started the climb to the mountain. But she dared not.

"Men and gods," she thought angrily, and at the same time was a little afraid of her thoughts, "men and gods—as if there are not bodies which need food and water to live and warmth to survive in the cold winds of the mountain heights. But then men do not make bodies, so what do they care about what bodies need?" She turned back toward the tent, casting a last look toward the mountains. But by now she could no longer discern Arrhal's figure against the lights and shadows of the slopes of the rising mountain. She slowly lay back down by her child, who was still deeply asleep, and she pulled him close to her, cherishing the warmth of the small body.

"Arrhal," she whispered, "Arrhal, beloved, take care of yourself. We need you more than all the gods there are," she added rebelliously. It took her a long time to warm herself enough to fall asleep, and all the while she kept thinking of Arrhal climbing the barren mountainside to meet the gods who had called him.

She woke in the morning in a cold and damp tent. A heavy fog had settled over the plateau, and people and horses and tents appeared and disappeared in the drifting fog, making the world unreal. Mirrha thought about Arrhal on the mountain and wondered if the fog had been sent by the gods to conceal their faces from the ordinary people. It was cold, and the fires did not burn well. The baby was coughing because the smoke would not rise and instead filled the tent.

Mirrha was tired and restless and finally carried the baby over to her mother's tent, where her little foster sister gladly took the baby and carried him around and around the tent. Nahru was only eleven summers, but her breasts had begun to bud this spring, and Mirrha felt certain that she would come into her womanhood before winter came to cover the plateau with its fierce winds and snow drifts.

Nahru had been taken into Mirrha's mother's tent when she was still a suckling babe, having lost her own mother from the summer fever. Mirrha's mother had put down Nete, Mirrha's chubby baby brother, and laid the wailing child on her other breast. She had had easily enough milk for the two, and the children had grown up together, playing and running and fighting together like all the other children.

When dusk fell over the valley, the fog had not lifted, and Mirrha's heart became heavy. Arrhal had not returned, and she dared not leave the tents, both for fear of the shaman's command and also because there was no way she could find the path to the mountain now.

She slept restlessly, with strange dreams troubling her sleep, and the baby woke three times, crying and demanding to be held and rocked. In the morning the fog began to lift, but the top of the mountain range was still covered with a heavy blanket of clouds, hanging nearly into the valley.

Mirrha spent much of the day sitting in front of the tent staring at the mountain range. The child continued to cry, and she could not find the patience in her to sooth him. Her mother, seeing her troubled state of mind, took the fussing boy from her. "Rest, child, and do not trouble yourself so. He will be back, your man. The gods only talk to men; they do not keep them."

In the afternoon she rose and went to the meadow where the tribe's horses were grazing. She sought out the brown mare that had been Arrhal's wedding present for her and greeted her.

The mare pushed her soft nose against Mirrha's hands, looking for the roots that she often brought. But today Mirrha had nothing for the mare. She thought of mounting the horse and riding to the mountain, but the warning of the shaman still sounded in her ears.

Mirrha went over to Arrhal's big black stallion, his head high as if listening to a call. His ears twitched for and back, and when she laid her hand on his strong neck, he shook himself a little as if not to be disturbed. "Are the gods talking to you too?" Mirrha whispered. But the stallion paid no attention to her.

She turned to see the shaman standing on a little hillock close to his tent. He stood very straight and still, his eyes fixed on the mountains and he, too, appeared to be listening.

The sun was beginning to set and the air was very still. There were no bird songs, and even the wind that never stopped whispering through the thin, dry grasses had ceased.

Mirrha sat on a small, smooth rock from which she could see the tribe's round tents and the mountainside. The fires had been lit for the evening meals and the smoke went straight into the air. The chomping of the grazing horses soothed her troubled heart, and after a while she lay down in the grass and stared into the slowly paling sky as it turned from a light bird's-egg green to shades of lavender.

The first star found Mirrha deeply asleep, and even the nuzzling of her brown mare did not wake her. It was close to midnight when she sat up bewildered, trying to remember how she had

184 IRENE B. SEELAND

come to sleep in the meadow, when a lightening flash crossed the sky above her. Some flashes moved within the clouds, lighting up the whole sky. Some stood like pillars of fire between heaven and earth, tearing the fabric of the air.

Thunderstorms were common in the valley but they almost always came in the spring or the summer, bringing the much-needed rain to the arid plains. But it was only when the flashes lit up the mountain range that Mirrha remembered Arrhal in the mountains talking to the gods.

"Gods, are you trying to instruct him or kill him?" she cried out, finding her way through the horses, which were now standing close together with their heads bent against the rain that began to move across the valley in great gray sheets of water.

Arrhal's stallion stood aside from the other horses, his head high and his nostrils drawing in the air that came from the mountains in long swells of wetness. Mirrha stroked his head:

"Take me to him," she whispered, "please, take me to him. He needs us both now." And the horse, which never allowed anybody but Arrhal to mount, stood still as she swung herself on his back.

She dared not ride him fast, because the thunderstorm had brought deep darkness to the valley, and the heavy clouds allowed only a little dim light of the moon to give them direction.

When they came to the foot of the mountain, Mirrha slid down from the wet animal. "Wait for us," she said. "I will bring him back to you." She found a crevice that allowed a quicker ascent into the rocks above her. The stones were sharp and slippery from the rain, and at times, the rainwater formed little runnels of ice-cold water quickly soaking her completely. Much of the time Mirrha had to crawl on hands and knees, finding the next holds above her by touch more than sight. She had only gained half the height of the mountain when the clouds began to break open above her, and although the depth of the crevice still lay in deep shadows, she could see the end of her climb bathed in silvery light.

She reached the top of the mountain with trembling legs, and when she straightened, she saw that she had torn her hands and knees on the rocks.

The valley lay below in the light of the moon. The last clouds were drawing away to the horizon, and the stars seemed so close that she felt she could touch them. It was much colder up here, and the wind cut through her wet leather tunic.

She stood quietly, searching the bare smooth rim of the mountain falling off steeply into the valley for any sign of Arrhal. It took her a little while to realize that what she had taken for an old tree stump beside a large boulder was a human figure.

Arrhal was sitting without any motion and, it appeared to her, without breath. As Mirrha approached him, she could see his eyes wide open, staring into the valley. He showed no sign of hearing her approach. She bent to him and laid her hand lightly on his arm. "Arrhal," she whispered, "come back to me, Beloved."

A small sound came from Arrhal, but no words. He turned his head toward her, and Mirrha, staring into his wide-open eyes, realized with sudden fear that they were sightless.

She cried out and cradled his head to her breast. And it was then, with the touch of her warmth and the life within her, that some semblance of life returned to Arrhal's body. He clung to her for a long time while she knelt beside him, rubbing his ice-cold limbs and finally helping him to stand. He was trembling like a man rising from a long sickbed, and he had to lean on her small, sturdy figure to take his first few steps.

Mirrha was afraid. How would she ever be able to take him back into the valley in his present weakness? But she turned toward the crevice, and half-supporting, half-carrying him, brought them to the edge of their descent.

She could never clearly remember afterwards how they had found their way down over the sharp, steep rocks, sometimes sliding, sometimes falling, but in the end, the crevice opened into a little space with grass where she let Arrhal down, holding his head in her lap, tears of exhaustion running over her face.

When she heard the sound of horses, she thought that the

stallion had found his way to them, but then she realized that there were three or four horses approaching. She tried to penetrate the deep shadows surrounding them, but it was only when the old voice of the shaman called Arrhal's name that she knew that they would be safe.

The shaman, with two other men of the tribe, had brought the makings for fire and food, and a gourd of the honey drink, and Arrhal's heavy fur cloak. The men stripped him of his wet clothing and rubbed his arms and legs with hot oils. The shaman heated the honey drink over the fire and stirred herbs into it, which filled the air with aromatic fragrances.

He poured some of the steaming drink into a small bowl and, moving stiffly on his thin bent legs, came to Mirrha, where she sat close to the small fire trying to dry her clothes. He smiled and his voice was gentle in spite of its roughness. "You did well, child," he said. "When the gods have finished talking to men, there is need of human love and warmth and food for the body. Arrhal has chosen well for his mate."

Mirrha looked at him. "His eyes," she asked fearfully, "what happened to his eyes? Will he see again?"

"Seeing the face of the gods strikes men blind," said the shaman, "but I trust that the gods do not want the leader of this tribe to be sightless for the rest of his days. We will keep him in a darkened tent for three days, and then we will know if his sight has returned."

Three days and nights Mirrha spent at Arrhal's side, the tent flaps closed, and during the days his eyes covered with a dark cloth as the shaman had instructed her. Arrhal did not speak much, but he was able to ask for water. Twice the shaman came and sat with him for a long while and sent Mirrha to care for her child.

In the morning of the fourth day, the shaman entered the tent with a bowl of a hot herbal brew sweetened with honey. He assisted Arrhal in sitting up and held the bowl to his lips. Mirrha, who had never seen the shaman perform any but the most sacred rites of her tribe, marveled at his gentleness.

The shaman removed the cloth that was tied to cover Arrhal's eyes: "Open your eyes slowly," he commanded. "The tent is dark and things may be blurred for a while."

Mirrha crouched beside the sleeping furs, holding her breath. Arrhal's eyes opened, and with a sigh of relief, he smiled. "I can see light, Yarhun." He laid his hand in a gesture of thanks on the old man's shoulder. The shaman rose, nodded to Mirrha with a small smile and left the tent.

Arrhal turned and took Mirrha's face between his strong brown hands. "Little one," he said, "little one," and then he buried his face on her shoulder and cried.

At the time of the next full moon, Arrhal and the shaman called the tribe together from the whole length of the valley to give them the teachings that Arrhal had been given by the gods on the mountain.

The teachings were strange and bewildering. Arrhal told them that the gods had chosen their tribe to learn a new way of living together. From now on, they would not use force to gain power or wealth, nor would they fight each other to settle matters of dispute or honor. Instead, they would choose from among themselves those they thought wisest, and ask for council in matters of disagreement and abide by the rulings of those chosen. Those who had greater riches of horses and sheep and other goods would see to it that those suffering from illness or age would be given not only enough to survive, but be fed and clothed with gifts given freely to those in need.

The men of the tribe shook their heads, some laughing, some angry. "What gods are these, that they want us to sit and talk like old women instead of measuring our strength in honest fight?" Ruhal, one of the younger chieftains, called out.

Mirrha, sitting with the other women and the smaller children to the side of the gathering, smiled. She knew Ruhal well, a handsome, spirited young man, high in the favor of women, who for a while had pursued her when she had become a woman. He was a good warrior but tended to use his strength too often in pursuit of his own pleasures.

Arrhal turned to him:" Too many good lives are lost in fighting over some sheep or the honor of a woman who does not care to guard it herself," he said. "There are those among us wise in years and experience. Let us choose twelve to meet together and among themselves think deeply about these matters. Let them tell us how to settle our disagreements and how to use our wealth for the benefit of all."

"But let me also say this now and for all times—and this is what the gods have commanded me to say. Let all those who will abide by the new teachings of the gods stay with the tribe of their father and their fathers before them. But let those who will not abide by them leave us now and join other tribes in other valleys. For if you stay here and disregard the new order which the gods have told us to live by, you will be put to death."

A sudden silence fell over the gathered tribe. Never before in time remembered had any man lost his life but by illness, accident or old age, in a fight with another member of the tribe, or in battle with other tribes.

Yet there was something in Arrhal's voice and his gaze that wandered slowly and deliberately over the assembled men and women that made Mirrha shiver as if a cold wind were blowing from the mountain. The others felt it too, and nobody dared to challenge Arrhal again.

Winter came, and with it hard times. Snow fell for many days, and the winds came howling down the mountain, blowing it like sand into large drifts. It was a long winter and the tribe had to slaughter more sheep than usual to feed its people. But the new rules of the gods were held to among the people, and fewer of the very young, the old, and the weak died than in previous winters.

Mirrha conceived again from Arrhal and was in her third month

when the spring winds came to the valley, the snows melted and
the meadows shimmered in the rich green of the first grass. The
ewes lambed and Mirrha and Nahru spent time with the herding
boys to watch the lambs trying to stand on their spindly legs, tails
wiggling with a life of their own as they found nourishment for
the first time.

Summer came, and Mirrha became heavier with child. Arrhal
left with two of the other chieftains to trade for metals and turquoise
in other valleys, and she felt lonely in the large tent. Terre, as they
had named their first son, toddled on sturdy legs among the tents
with the other children and was watched by the old women too
frail to help with carrying water from the river or gathering firewood.

It was during the height of summer that Mirrha and Nahru
took a skin of water and some dried meal cakes and set out at dawn
towards the mountains to make an offering to the gods for the
birth and health of Mirrha's child. The cliff side of the mountain
range had become a sacred place to the tribe since the time the
gods had spoken to Arrhal there. And the women of the tribe had
found a small spring to make their offerings to the moon goddess
who guards the mothers and the births of children.

They let their horses ride at ease and by noontime came to the
crevice leading into the mountain. Mirrha was glad to slide down
from her mare and settled herself against a rock. Her back was
aching and, after a while, she lay down in the shadow of an old
gnarled fir tree that grew among the boulders that had tumbled
from the mountainside. Nahru, restless and not burdened with a
child in her womb, wandered off in search of berries.

Mirrha was awakened from her peaceful slumber by Nahru's
screaming. She came to her feet too fast and had to steady herself
against a sudden spell of dizziness. She could hear Nahru crying
for help, but the echo in the rocks made it hard for her to find a
direction.

She finally found an entrance to another crevice leading from the main one into the mountain to her right. She ran, calling Nahru's name, having to stop now and again to press her hand to her side, where a sharp pain caught her breath.

The crevice turned at a sharp angle, and when Mirrha entered into the shadowy rocks, she saw Nahru huddled on the ground, her tunic torn. There were bloodstains on the grass around her and on her clothes.

Mirrha ran up to her and, in running, scanned the rocks and the scraggly bushes growing in small patches for any sign of predators. There were mountain lions living in those rocks, and she had seen some of the men bring home their soft yellow furs. It was then that she saw Ruhal standing in the shadows, holding his big brown stallion who was stamping restlessly trying to move away from the smell of the blood.

Mirrha stared at Ruhal, who with an arrogant smile mounted his horse and tried to press by the two women. She stood up and held the horse by its reins. "Did you force yourself on this child?" Mirrha asked, her voice shaking with fury.

Ruhal looked down at her. "She is not a child any longer, and if she did not want to be taken, she should not smile at a grown man the way she smiled at me." With that he pressed his heels into the flanks of the horse and, pulling the reins from Mirrha's hands, rode the horse from the small glen in a fast canter.

Mirrha knelt by the girl and held her close to her breast. "Cry, little sister," she murmured, "cry if it will ease your heart. But I swear by the goddess that no woman of this tribe shall be forced to submit to any man not of her own choosing."

Dusk was falling over the valley when the two women finally reached the tents of the tribe. Mirrha helped Nahru from her horse, led her to her mother's tent and, after bedding the shivering girl in warm fur covers, went to seek the woman who had helped her in childbirth.

The young moon was standing high in the clear night sky when Mirrha came to her tent. She let herself fall on to her sleeping furs, too tired to eat. Terre was deep asleep in the corner of the tent, holding a round little arm over the puppy that had attached itself to him recently. In spite of her misery and anger, Mirrha had to smile. The two young ones were so alike in their complete abandonment to sleep. She was just falling asleep, when she heard steps coming up to the tent and Arrhal entered. She began to rise, but he knelt beside her and held her close in his arms.

"I am glad to be back," he said. "We traveled farther than we planned and we met people from strange lands and traded for things of great beauty. But before we can share in all the things that I have seen and heard on my travels, I need to know what has happened here today that has brought the people to whispering and Nahru to crying and has made your face sad with pain."

Then Mirrha clung to him and wept, and told him how she had found Nahru torn and bleeding, and how Ruhal had ridden away, blaming the girl herself for the assault.

Arrhal's face darkened and his eyes looked into the night toward the mountains. "I will call the elders together in the morning and we will call Ruhal to explain his action," he said quietly. "No man may force a woman to submit to him against her will. In the past, her father or brother would have challenged Ruhal in battle for this. I am the closest male relation to her, being your husband, with her father dead these past three years. Gladly would I have stood for her in battle. But I myself am bound by the laws of the gods."

He pressed her back into the furs. "Sleep, my love," he said. "I will have word with Yarhun tonight and sit with him in prayer, that we may find the wisdom for right action."

In the morning the elders met in council for a long time by the tent of the shaman. Mirrha woke late and found that a messenger had been sent in the night to the tents of Ruhal's people, who were grazing their herds at the other end of the valley.

Ruhal rode in at late morning, accompanied by his younger brother and the brother of his mother. He sat straight on his horse, and when he dismounted, he threw the reins to the little horse

boy with an arrogance that brought the anger back to Mirrha's
heart.

The elders questioned Ruhal at length, and also listened to
the report of Myra, the midwife who had tended to Nahru's injuries.

Then the elders met alone for what seemed to Mirrha a long
time. In the end they called the people of the tribe together to
hear their pronouncement over Ruhal, who had forced a girl barely
come into her womanhood against her will, inflicting serious injury
that might leave her scarred for life and unable to bear children to
a man of her choice.

The oldest of the elders, a man related to Mirrha's mother by
marriage to her sister stood in front of the others.

"Last year we were chosen by the gods to live with a new order
among ourselves and we agreed to do so. None have chosen to
leave as we had the freedom to do. Today, we have to pronounce
judgment on one who under the old order would have been
challenged to battle by a male member of the woman's family. It is
our will that he be put to death by the arrows of twelve men of the
tribes of this valley. The twelve will be those who take a white
stone from this bowl I hold in my hands."

The men stood in silence for a few moments. Then they
advanced slowly one by one to take a stone from the bowl and give
it to the shaman who took it from them. The foreheads of those
who had picked a white stone, he marked with oil mixed with
white clay.

Ruhal had stood throughout the whole process like one stunned
by a blow. Now he turned to Arrhal, and in his eyes was a question.
Mirrha who stood by Arrhal, shivered. Her heart that had been
filled with so much anger ached at the sight of the despair in the
eyes of the man who had thought he was to die in battle like a
warrior, and now saw himself to be slaughtered like a lamb. She
grasped at Arrhal's hand.

"Is there no other way?" she whispered. He looked down at
her sadly. "We are here to bring the new law," he said, "and we are
bound to uphold it."

"But is this new law better than the old?" Mirrha's eyes were drawn back to Ruhal's frozen face. "Is it better for a man to die like a sheep going to slaughter than fight an honest fight?"

"In a fight, the one who is strongest of body will win. That was good when strength of body was necessary for the survival of a tribe. Now the time has come where the tribes are to grow in strength of will and in caring for one another. So the law of the strongest no longer holds true. It is hard for men to change the ways they learned from their fathers and their fathers before them. But just as a babe grows into a child and a child into a man learning new skills and new responsibilities, so the tribes have to grow and learn new responsibilities and new tasks."

"What will be the end of the learning?" Mirrha's eyes searched his face with great seriousness. "Will there ever be an end to change and new learning?"

Arrhal smiled. "Not for a long time, little wise one. There will be generations and generations just mastering this new lesson, and many others to come. But one day, one day so far away that you and I cannot imagine it, man will understand himself and know his source and his destiny as the gods know it now."

He led Mirrha to their tent where her mother was guarding the child. But when he bent to kiss her and turned to pick up his hunting bow, Mirrha knew with some consolation whose arrow would be the surest to find Ruhal's heart.

*   *   *

Mirrha opened her eyes and looked around her. The angel sat down beside her and took her hand. "Welcome back," he smiled.

Mirrha gazed at his face. "I have never seen you before and yet I feel that I know you," she said timidly.

"We have known each other for all eternity," the angel replied, "and yet each time you return, it seems like the first time for you!"

"I fell asleep in front of my tent. I was so tired from a fever that had entered my body. What has happened to me?" Mirrha wondered.

"Your body was very old and tired, and it was time for you to leave it behind," the angel said kindly, and patted her hand reassuringly.

"Is this then the place where the gods dwell that spoke to Arrhal?" she asked.

"No," the angel replied, "this is the place where all souls dwell for a while before they start on their next journey."

"Ah," said Mirrha and was silent for a while. The angel looked at her with fondness. "You did well, in this life, little friend," he added softly. "You carried many burdens and faithfully fulfilled all the responsibilities that were yours. You did well."

"It was hard after Arrhal was killed, when the raiders came," Mirrha sighed. "I missed him so much. But our sons were nearly grown and the other men in the village helped us. It was good that we had the new laws; otherwise they would have fought over me as the wife of the chief. In this way I did not have to have another man and could grow old in peace. It was good," and she smiled.

"Did the tribe continue to follow the laws after Arrhal died?" the angel asked.

"Oh yes, they had seen how much better life had become for everybody and that we all benefited from it. Even other tribes, which had at first mocked our men for not fighting anymore over everything, began to see the wisdom of these laws and started to follow them. It was good," she said again and nodded to herself.

The angel looked at her for a long while as she sat peacefully looking around.

"Your tribe started something very new and very important," he said. "It will be of great importance for a long time to come, and it will allow for many new things to develop, now that people are beginning to live in greater peace and cooperation."

"What kind of things?" Mirrha looked at him curiously.

"There will be time for new learning. People will begin to try to understand the laws of nature; they will begin to see the beauty of nature around them and begin to imitate some of it. Living together in greater peace and harmony will make all this possible."

"I had started to carve patterns on some clay pots I made, like I saw on the skin of snakes. Is that what you mean?"

"Yes, that is the beginning," the angel nodded.

"The shaman had started to make pictures on sheep skins to tell about our lives, and he also began to make marks on them for the seasons as they passed, so we could show the young ones what had happened to the tribe in the past."

The angel smiled: "That, too, is the beginning of the new learning," he said. "It will take many forms in the future, this keeping records, but it will be important for humankind to know about its history."

"So what Arrhal did was important?" Mirrha asked shyly.

"Very important," the angel confirmed. "In every generation there are always a few who can envision the need of the future and bring it to their people. Arrhal was fortunate that his people listened to him and followed him, even though they did not always understand or even agree. But they trusted him and later saw that it was good. This has formed a bond among all of you that will make it possible to live and work together again in the future. There have been others in the past and there will be more in the future who will be rejected and even slain for the new teachings they bring, yet their sacrifice will make it possible for people to accept them in the end."

"Is Arrhal here?" Mirrha looked at the angel and her face showed her longing and her hope.

The angel shook his head. "He has gone on to his next task," he said kindly. "You know how he is. He cannot sit still and wait, and you had yet a long life to live. But you will see him again soon."

"Is he coming back here?" Mirrha wondered.

The angel laughed: "Everybody always comes back here, little friend. This is home! You journey for a while, but you will ever return to your true home."

"It is lovely here," Mirrha sighed happily and closed her eyes again.

The angel looked at her fondly. "Yes," he said softly, "it is lovely here, precious little soul. How could it not be?" And he, too, closed his eyes for a while.

EPILOGUE

The sun was sinking toward the western hills. The hawk had drifted into the valley on the evening wind, and now the liquid song of the wood thrush was the only sound filling the woods around the house. The old woman pulled her silver gray shawl closer around her shoulders. The house was quiet. "They must have gone to the cliff to see the sunset," she thought, and in her mind's eye saw them sitting on the bare gray slabs of rock, watching as the sun sank toward the horizon. The view from up there had always been spectacular, and they had spent many sunsets in all seasons on those cliffs, talking together, singing or just being silent together.

She thought of them all with love and gratefulness, the friends who had gathered around Ethan in this life, who had stayed together to live and grow and learn and work in ever-growing kinship of their souls. She thought of them as she had remembered them through the different lives, through the many ages. She thought of their shared times of joy and of despair, the seasons of love, of birth, and of death they had experienced together. She remembered the times of learning and growing, the times when the challenge of life had been confronted with courage, and the times when fear and doubt had led to missed opportunities.

She was grateful that the recollection of all those other lives had brought her to a deeper understanding of their various relationships, the different ways they had known each other over many lives—as parents and children, lovers and friends, teachers and disciples, lords and servants, rich and poor, high born and lowly, and she knew with certainty that there would be many more times when they would come together and join their energy and talents and love to bring into realization the growing unity of humankind.

She smiled as she realized how for some, the strength of their past experiences had carried over into this life: Phillipus, now a senior executive, still looked more like a Roman soldier; Nahru, born into a wealthy family, had left to live with Native Americans; Mara and Petronius were again the devoted couple she remembered with so much love. Marius, still preferring brown clothes to any other, again was a close and beloved friend. And she also saw how past debts and missed opportunities had come to closure in this life.

The sun was standing low over the horizon now, a great golden globe irradiating the edges of the few summer clouds gathered in the transparent evening sky that flamed behind the cliffs, setting them on fire. The old woman leaned back in her chair. The wind had died down and ceased its timeless whispering in the pine trees.

A movement outside her vision made her turn her head. She saw a figure dimly, standing quietly in the gathering shadows below the stone arches. She closed her eyes and opened them again. She could feel her heart beating rapidly, as if she had been running. The sinking sun cast its last golden rays through a cloudbank, and then she knew his face—golden and radiant like the sun.

"You came back, my love. After all these years, you came back for me!"

His voice was soft but very clear, and its sound made her heart ache with longing.

"I promised you I would be back. But then—I was never far away, my love. I was with all of you, always." He laughed and came towards her and reached out to her.

Her heart fluttered and stumbled and became still. There was a moment of vertigo and then a burst of radiant light. She rose from her body lightly and joyfully, and together they moved toward the fire on the mountain, to follow the sun on its journey toward the next sunrise.

*   *   *

The old woman gazed at the angel with fondness. "You again," she smiled, "I remember you!"

"Finally," the angel laughed, "and about time, too. I thought you would never learn to remember!"

"I remembered so much in this last life," she said and sighed. "So many of my past lives, the lessons learned, the many mistakes, over and over, the opportunities missed. It was painful sometimes to remember all this, but it also helped to see the patterns in order not to repeat them again."

"Yes," the angel nodded. "Your soul helped you to remember so that you could make better choices this time."

She laughed. "I think I broke some of the patterns this time. I did not run away again when things got hard. I did not refuse to take on my responsibilities, although at times they seemed a bit overwhelming."

"They were," the angel confirmed. "You chose it to be so. You wanted to finish up with the old burdens this time to clear up your slate for new things. And you did. Many of the old debts are paid and balanced. You will be able to make freer choices next time with fewer conditions and limitations. There were quite a few challenges this time: your being born during war times; your poor health as a child; the absence of a father; your irresistible urge to become a doctor; Ethan's early death leaving you as a young widow with a child and with so many responsibilities—all this was part of what you chose for this life."

"What was I thinking!" she muttered under her breath, and then laughed. "It was a bit ambitious. No wonder I despaired at times!"

"But you managed it well, and you did succeed with what you had chosen."

"Well," she said, "It was also a very rich life. I met so many wonderful people who were working hard to bring some light and hope to our planet. There has been so much change for the good in my lifetime, along with all the terrible and stupid things that happened. I was always a bit of a pessimist. But somehow this has changed. I know now how great a difference each person of truly good will can make. It has given me hope, even during the dark times."

She sat for a while as she reflected on what she just had recalled. Then she shook herself a little.

"Well, it is done," she said. "What happens now?"

"What would you like to happen?" the angel asked, and his face had a quizzical expression.

"Oh, for heaven's sake!" she exclaimed. "You sound like me when I dealt with my patients. Please, not here, too!"

"No, seriously," the angel said, "it really is up to you now. You are quite free to choose what happens in your next life."

She sat and thought for a while. "What are the others up to?" she asked and looked around. "Those who got here before me. I would like to sit down with them and talk it over."

"Good," said the angel, "I hoped you would ask for them. They are waiting for you, and I will take you to them shortly. Yet you must have some desire for yourself."

She shook her head. "No, not really," she answered quietly. "Whatever needs doing the most."

"Well," the angel said, "you truly have learned much this time." And he reached out his hand to help her up.

"Wait!" she said, "before we go to meet the others! Tell me, who are you?"

"Don't you know?" the angel gazed at her, and she felt as if she was falling into the depth of the starry heavens.

She was silent for a long while. And then she smiled. "You have always been here when I returned. You have always helped me understand the lessons of my life. You have always been so wise, so loving even when you were frustrated with me. I felt you were older than time, and yet timeless. But right now I can't help remembering that funny old story—I wonder if you know it? About the earthworm who met his other end, and fell in love with it?"

The angel groaned: "Look, I did ask you to develop a sense of humor, but this?"

"Well," she said, "you asked for it." They both laughed.

"Yes," she added quietly, "yes, I know you now!"

And she rose to step into the angel's open arms, and as his wings enfolded her, they became one.

*

* * *

* * * * *